His to Hold

ISBN: 978-1-9995736-6-9

Editor: Brandi Aquino, Editing Done Write

Cover Design: Thunderstruck Cover Designs

Dedicated to my husband

May we always have a plate of meatballs and chocolate chip cookies to get us through all the stressful times.

Chapter One

Bryce

I walked into the office Friday morning and, having gotten only three hours of sleep the night before, knew I looked like shit. Staying up arguing with your ex because she doesn't feel the need to leave your condo takes its toll. We had broken up months ago, and I had taken pity because she had nowhere to go, but now she was just being an unreasonable bitch.

I probably wouldn't have even come in today, but Hunter and Carter had called a last-minute meeting with Chase and me. I had no choice but to go in. I was hoping to sign on as junior partner this year and it would look bad if I hadn't shown up. My brothers had gotten nothing handed to them, and they believed in making me work for what I wanted.

Chase and I had been working with one of our top clients on a corporate merger. They were looking at buying a smaller local company, but upon thorough review of the books, things weren't looking consistent. Our client wanted a second opinion, and I couldn't say I blamed him.

I entered the office carrying a hot cup of coffee and a bag containing a breakfast sandwich from the coffee shop around the corner from my place. I didn't have the time or desire to eat at home. Alyssa wasn't even up out of bed when I left, and I knew if I hung around and took my time, she would start on me as soon as she was awake.

I glanced at my watch. I was on limited time, and as soon as this meeting was finished, I needed to start preparing for my own upcoming meetings today. My phone hadn't stopped going off all morning, starting as soon as I had turned it on. I greeted Josie and Kim and entered through the doors of our boardroom. I took a seat beside Carter, who had his head down in the client file.

"Morning," I mumbled, sitting down and unwrapping my breakfast, running my hand over my face.

"About time you got here." He chuckled. "I see you got the breakfast of champions this morning."

"Yeah, I know. Sorry I'm late. Alyssa still hasn't left. She is making my life a living hell."

"You really should deal with that, instead of hoping she just goes away."

"It's not like I haven't tried," I said, taking a bite of my sandwich and ignoring what my brother said. He knew the troubles I had been and still was having with her, and he knew how hard I had tried to get rid of her. I took another bite and downed it with a mouthful of coffee as Chase walked in carrying a cup of coffee and sat on the other side of Carter.

"Jesus, you're just as bad as Bryce," Carter said, closing the client file and looking to Chase.

"Yeah, well, it was a late night, if you catch my drift." Chase smiled smugly.

"We don't want to hear about your latest conquest. It's a business day. Save that for guys' night," Carter said, clearing his throat and diving right in. "Hunter had an early appointment this morning, so he won't be here."

Carter cleared his throat again and jumped into all of the company business as usual. "All right, so I did manage to get a minute to look over some of the case files you two are working on, especially the one you asked me to look over, and I know you want a second opinion," he said, shuffling some papers around.

"So, here's the problem: There is something definitely up with the new documents your client was given. Your client is right to think something is going on. Things are not consistent. So, you guys are going to advise your client to request a meeting with TexCorp. You are both going to go over those documents firsthand at that meeting and request any other documents that you see fit that will support the documents here. Chase, according to your email, the meeting has been set for four weeks from Monday, is that correct?"

Chase nodded.

I pulled my phone out of my pocket and pulled up my calendar. "The tenth of February?" I questioned.

"Yep, eight in the morning."

I updated my calendar with the meeting details.

"Chase, send over the details to Bryce," Carter ordered. "Bottom line, your client feels that they are lying about something, and I agree, so it's up to the two of you to figure it out. He wants a second set of eyes on everything before he enters into the contract."

"Fair enough." I stood. "If that is everything, I need to get to my office."

"Yes, that's it. Have a good day, boys," Carter said as we both left the boardroom.

Chase and I parted ways, him going into his office just around the corner from the boardroom. I continued down the hall, and as soon as I rounded the corner to my office, I was immediately attacked with questions. I wasn't in the mood this morning for this, and I barked out orders and answers left and right a lot harsher than I normally would.

I had just gotten into my office, shut the door, and sat down, when Kim, my legal assistant, came in and handed me the file that she had been working on for a meeting I was to have on Friday. She didn't say anything. She laid the file on my desk and left quietly, while I listened to my voice mail.

Of course, the first message I had was from Alyssa. I rolled my eyes as I listened to her whine, and by the time I hit that last message and her voice came over the speaker again, it pissed me off more than I already was. I let out a breath as I hung up the phone, trying to regain my composure.

Once I had calmed down enough, I opened the file that Kim had left for me and began going through all the paperwork she had completed. Every page I looked at was nothing but a half-assed attempt at putting together information for me. Everything about it was wrong. I pressed the intercom, calling her into my office. I waited, drumming my pen on the edge of the desk.

"Mr. Malone, you wanted to see me?" she meekly announced as I sat behind my desk, highly agitated and pissed off.

"I did. Please, come in and sit down." I nodded to the chair across from me. My eyes followed her as she shyly walked in and took a seat in the chair. She folded her shaking hands in her lap and looked at me.

"In regard to these documents. What the fuck are you

thinking? I can't go into a meeting with these clients with this type of drivel," I said, throwing the paperwork around.

I could see the tears welling in her eyes, but I didn't care.

"Sir, I completed everything as—"

I held my hand up to stop her. "If you dare say you completed everything as I would want it, you may collect your things and head home right now.".

Her lip started to tremble. I glanced out my office door and saw Josie walk by my office, glaring at me, at my behavior and utter lack of professionalism.

I got up and slammed my office door shut. I had already had it out with Josie today as well, before I had even come into the office this morning. I had zero professionalism today, along with zero patience, and I knew it.

I collected the mass of paperwork, shoving it back into the file, and handed it to Kim. "Fix it," I barked out, and turned my attention to another file sitting on my desk.

She stood there looking at me, not knowing what to say or do.

"I suggest you get to work. You have many hours of it to do, and you aren't going to get it done by standing there staring at me," I barked.

She hid it well, but I could see a tremble in her lower lip before she quickly turned and left my office. I was sure I would have a complaint filed to Carter and Hunter in a matter of minutes for how I had just treated her. If that happened, I was sure my shot at junior partner would be put in jeopardy, and it would be just one more thing I could blame Alyssa for. After all, she was the reason behind my delightful attitude.

Before I opened my next file, I went to take a sip of my coffee, finding it had gone cold, which set me off even more. Mug in hand, I walked down to the coffee room. Employees were stepping out of my way, whispering to one another, as I walked down the hall, most turning their faces away from me, but no one dared speak to me with the way I was behaving.

As soon as I walked in, I saw Kim in the corner with Josie. She took one look at me, wiped her eyes with her thumb, and left the room, along with every employee in there, except one—Josie. She had been my personal assistant since I became a lawyer here. She knew me better than most of the staff, aside from my brothers. She, like them, was not afraid to call me on my shit.

"Bryce, may I have a few words with you in your office when you are finished here." She didn't give me a chance to reply. She turned on her heal and marched out of the room, no doubt, heading down the hall to my office.

With a fresh cup of hot coffee in hand, I made my way back to my office. When I entered, Josie sat in the chair across from me, drumming her fingers on my desk.

"What is it?" I barked.

"Bryce, I have just spoken to Kim. I have talked her out of reporting you to HR and to your brothers, so essentially I just saved your ass. What is wrong with you? You don't act this way."

"Nothing."

She looked at me in disbelief. I knew it because she was right. I never acted this way.

"Bryce, you better get your shit together. I looked at Kim's work before she submitted it to you. There was absolutely nothing wrong with it. Now, if this is a personal issue between yourself and her, then I suggest you have a talk with Carter or Hunter and get her transferred. You cannot and will not be abusive to staff. I won't allow it. Do I make myself clear?"

One thing about Josie that I had always admired was she never cared if she stepped out of turn. She was right. She was saving my ass, and for that I was thankful.

"I mean it, Bryce, and if it's a personal issue outside of this building, then you best go home and straighten it out before you get yourself into trouble."

"Send Kim in," I grumbled.

"Are you going to be rational?" she asked.

"I said, send her in."

Josie looked at me, shook her head, and left without another word.

Ten minutes later, Kim appeared at my door, file in

hand. She was just about to sit down when my phone buzzed on my desk.

"Put the file on my desk and I will review it once again."

"Mr. Malone, if I have done something wrong, please tell me."

"It's not you, Kim. Leave the file. I am giving you the rest of the day off with pay to make up for my behavior. Go to this address." I quickly scribbled the address of the day spa Hunter and Carter sent their wives, Autumn and Hope, to and handed it to her. "Have whatever treatments you would like and send the bill to me."

I'd probably be up shit creek for doing this, but I handed her the slip of paper anyway. She quickly took the paper from my hand and left my office without another word.

It was 10 p.m. by the time I had decided to head back to Chase's apartment. I had decided to stay there going forward, until Alyssa vacated my condo. I entered his condo to find all the lights off. No doubt Chase was either out or had some broad over.

I kicked my shoes off and loosened my tie and threw

my suit jacket down over the back of the couch. I made my way into the kitchen. I needed something to eat.

Pulling the fridge open, I grabbed the veggie tray and quickly made up a plate. After I ate, I made my way down to the spare bedroom. I changed and crawled into bed, then laid there with my arm over my face, letting the tensions of the day leave my body.

I had just about drifted off to sleep when I heard a woman moan Chase's name, and then the rhythmic sound of his headboard banging on the wall above my head. Last thing I wanted to listen to was my brother banging some broad.

I closed my eyes, trying to ignore the sound, but it just kept getting louder. I got up and pounded on the wall. "Trying to sleep in here, fuckface!" I shouted. I didn't care. If I couldn't be happy, why should he?

The rhythmic sound stopped, only to start again a few seconds later, and kept going until she was moaning and screaming his name even louder than before.

I rolled my eyes. I was irritated as hell, not to mention horny. With every bang of the headboard, I too wished I could sink myself into someone. I lay there for a few more minutes, and when I couldn't take it anymore, I got up out of bed and slid my suit pants back on, grabbed my shirt and jacket, and went back to the office.

Chapter Two

Bryce - A week later

"Bryce. Wake the fuck up."

I felt someone shove my shoulder. I opened my eyes, squinting at the light that was already pouring in through the windows of my office. What time was it, and what had happened last night?

As soon as I moved, I felt a searing pain run through my head. I blinked hard, Hunter and Carter coming into focus, both standing above me, frowning. What the hell were they doing here?

"What...what time is it?" I yawned, sitting up, rubbing my temples.

"It's seven-thirty. What the fuck is going on in here?

This office is a disaster," Hunter said as Carter took a minute to pick up the plastic food containers that were strewn about on the floor.

"Have you been living here?" Carter asked, looking annoyed.

I saw him looking at the clothes that hung in the corner of my office. I ran my hand over my face, trying to sit my sorry ass up. I had tied one on last night, getting too drunk to be able to drive back to Chase's condo.

"Yeah that is what Josie suspects," Hunter answered.

I'd had enough. Alyssa still wouldn't leave the condo, and all Chase was interested in was fucking women all hours of the night. I didn't know what the fuck was going on. I also didn't know what I had done wrong. It wasn't like either of them hadn't lived at the office at one point in their careers.

"You know Kim came to my office the other day to complain, right?" Carter told Hunter.

"Yeah, she called my office, but I was in with a client and had to leave right after that meeting. What was all that about?"

"Apparently, he gave her shit, and then paid her to take the day off. He then sent her to the spa, some form of bribe perhaps."

They were talking amongst themselves as if I wasn't even in the room.

"Fuck, it's enough!" I shouted, rubbing my hand over

my face and sitting up, my head still pounding, the room spinning.

"Bryce, what the fuck is going on?"

Both of my brothers stood looking at me. Thank God I had put my pants back on before passing out last night or this would have looked way worse than what it already did.

I cracked my neck, sat up, and looked toward the door. Josie walked by my office door on her way to her desk. She looked in quickly, and when she saw Hunter and Carter standing there, and then me staring back at her, she picked up her pace.

"Bryce, are you going to answer us?"

I really had nothing to say, except that I hated everything about my life at this exact moment. I looked to the garbage can filled with takeout containers, the empty bottle of booze that lay sideways on my desk, and the clothes that hung on hangers on the corner of my bookcase. "It's nothing."

My brothers looked at one another and then sat down. "We don't think so, Bryce. Spill it."

As more people began to pour into the office, Hunter got up and shut my office door and pulled the blinds on the windows that were open toward the hallway to give us more privacy.

"For God's sake, throw a shirt on, would you? Have some sort of respect for yourself," Carter demanded and threw a dirty, balled-up shirt at me that had been thrown in the corner earlier in the week.

"Surely you have not had clients in this office?" Carter asked.

I shook my head and threw my shirt on. "No, no clients."

"Did you actually bribe Kim?" Hunter asked, looking at me, waiting for my response.

I put my head in my hands. "Kind of," I whispered, running my hands over my face again.

"I don't think I need to tell you how against our policy that is, do I?" Carter barked.

"No, I already know. It was a mistake."

"Are you sleeping with her?" Hunter asked, picking up another container off the floor and throwing it into the garbage.

"What?" I gasped. "Are you serious?" Where the fuck did that thought come from? Who did he think I was, my brother?

"Are you sleeping with your paralegal? Because that is even more against our policies than I care to admit," Carter barked.

"Lord no. Fuck, I made a mistake, but I am not stupid enough to stick my dick into one of our employees."

"Bryce, this is warning number one."

Carter was never one to fuck around. He was always all business, and seriously, I knew better.

"I'm aiming for junior partner here. You actually think I would sleep with my paralegal? I don't fucking believe it." I jumped up off the couch and paced around my office.

"I wouldn't have thought you would bribe an employee either, to be honest," Carter answered.

"Look, I'd had a shitty day. I looked over the documents she had prepared and took shit out on her that had nothing to do with her. She bitched at Josie, who fucking told me, so I gave her the day off, treated her to a spa treatment. I didn't think I did anything wrong. I certainly didn't think she would lodge a fucking complaint," I said, throwing the almost empty bottle of liquor into the bottom drawer of my desk.

"As I said, that is warning number one," Carter repeated.

"Shove your fucking warning, Carter." I took a step toward him, but Hunter stepped between us. "All right, Bryce, calm the fuck down." He placed a firm hand on my chest and looked me in the eyes, reading what was there.

"Carter, how about you go and grab us some coffees and muffins from the bakery downstairs. Let me talk to Bryce for a second," he said, not taking his eyes from mine.

Carter didn't argue. I could tell he was fed up, which he should be. He was the one who started this firm and decided to pull each one of us in. He got up and left my office, shutting the door behind him, not once making eye contact with me. I looked at Hunter, him at me.

"Now you are going to sit down and tell me what is going on?"

"It's nothing."

"Oh no, no way. You think because I get rid of Carter, I'm letting you off the hook? Now sit down and explain yourself."

I was just about to start telling him when Josie knocked on my door. Hunter got up and walked over, pulling the door open. She looked over his shoulder directly at me and shook her head before turning her attention back to Hunter. "Carter called. He said you have an appointment downstairs, Hunter."

"Thanks, Josie."

Josie walked away and Hunter turned to me.

"I already know this has to do with Alyssa and you. I know things aren't good, Bryce. I also understand how hard it is to get your shit together after you've broken it off with someone you were planning to marry. Has she left your condo yet?"

It was like my brother was a mind reader. I leaned back against the couch and let out a breath. "No. I've been staying with Chase, but I am tired of listening to him bang anything with a heartbeat."

Hunter looked at me and chuckled. He glanced around the room and back to me, a look of pity coming to his eyes. "Get your office cleaned up, take the rest of today off, and effective immediately, you are on vacation. Two weeks," he said, pointing to me. "Get your clothes out of here too. Tell Alyssa she has two weeks to move or you will have her legally removed. Go up to the lake house, alone, and sort your shit out. You hear me."

"I can't. I have appointments this afternoon."

"No, you don't, not anymore. I'll have Josie reschedule them. I am doing this for your own good, and if I find out that you don't leave, I will have her change your passwords too so you can't access anything."

I rolled my eyes and watched Hunter leave my office. As irritated as I was, he was right. I needed a break. The last six months had gotten to me. I couldn't say I was sad over my breakup. Just more frustrated at the fact that she was torturing me because I had taken pity on her the night she started to cry when I told her she had to leave. Feeling sorry for her had gotten me to the point I was at.

I started gathering my things and cleaning my office. I didn't waste any time. I packed up all of my clothes, piled the garbage neatly in the bin, grabbed my laptop, and shut the lights off, heading down to the parking lot to my car.

The condo was quiet when I entered.

"Hello?" I called out. Silence was the only thing that greeted me.

I noticed a few boxes sat partially packed up on the dining room table. Thank goodness. That meant Alyssa was packing her shit.

I dropped the mess of clothes I carried in my arms into

the laundry hamper and walked over to the couch and flopped down. I leaned my head back against the cushions and pinched the bridge of my nose. The tension of the morning sat firmly planted in my neck and upper back.

I only sat for a few minutes before getting up and going down to the bedroom. I pulled my suitcase from the closet and quickly packed two weeks worth of clothes, then booked myself a late-afternoon flight. I went into my office and pulled a sheet of paper off one of my legal pads and quickly wrote: Alyssa, you have two weeks to get out. I'm done.

I dropped the sheet of paper on the table by her boxes, grabbed my bags, and locked the door.

Chapter Three

Mia

I sat behind my desk dreaming of the ocean as I hit print on my computer. I had spent the last two weeks preparing for today. It was so close I could taste it. I could already feel the heat from the sun on my skin, if I thought about it hard enough. I was anxious and excited, and I seriously couldn't wait until tonight. Not only was I going on vacation, but I got to spend the whole week with Don.

After five long years together and doing our best to make the long-distance relationship work between us, I was sure that this trip would be the one. He was going to pop the question; I just knew it. I could feel it. Sure, we had been having problems with the distance thing, as anyone would, and he had kept asking me to move down with him, but I kept putting him off.

One night, Don expressed his feelings about the issues we had been having. He felt neglected, so we began planning this trip and working on us. We hoped it would help our relationship, and so six months ago I had put in for this time off. It had been fifteen years since my last vacation, and I seriously didn't think it would get approved. Mark, my boss, never allowed me time off. Don had told me that I should just take it to him, so that was what I did. He finally granted it—begrudgingly, of course.

The printer rang out the telltale beeps that it was finally finished printing the documents, and I grabbed the reports for Mark. I bundled them together, securing them with a clip, and carried them down the hall to his office, stopping outside to take a breath. With the pending merger, I was petrified that at any given moment, he would take back the approval on my vacation.

I knocked and pushed the door open, entering the room. He was seated behind his desk, typing away.

"Here you go. Just what you asked for." I set the stack of data on his desk.

He picked them up and flipped through them, nodding his head. "Yes...yes, these look so much better, Mia. See, I told you a few simple tweaks would be all it would take, not to mention it would make all the difference."

"Uh huh," I gritted out. I hated being bullied into doing something that was wrong. Last night when Mark called me at home, after I had already given him all the data, he told me I would need to make things "look better," so he asked me to make a few adjustments. The conversation had ended with the threat of, "You don't want to lose your job, do you?" So to avoid a huge argument, I had just done what he had asked instead.

"Yes, this is exactly what I am talking about. See, you even put the company back in the black. This couldn't be more perfect, Mia."

"Uh huh, that is what you essentially wanted, wasn't it?"

Mark looked up from the reports and studied me.

"Mia, is there a problem?"

"No, nothing at all. Let me know if you need anything else before I leave," I answered, turning on my heel and walking out of his office.

While on my way back to my office, I stopped in the staff room and grabbed a cup of coffee, and my empty lunch bag from the fridge. I just wanted to be able to grab everything and go once 5:00 p.m. hit.

"Looking forward to vacation, Mia?" Janet asked.

"I am. I can't wait. I can't wait to sit under palm trees, put my feet in the hot sand, and drink margaritas."

"You deserve it, putting up with Mark and his demanding ways every day for the past five years. I'm surprised you have lasted this long. The girl before you only made it six months, and the one before her only three."

I smiled and added a little sugar to my coffee. I was overworked. A company this size should have had eight people in my department. Instead everything fell onto my shoulders.

"I'll see you later, Janet. I got to get some things finished before I leave." I didn't want to hear from someone else how much of a sucker I was. I already knew.

I took my coffee and made my way to my office, shutting the door behind me. I sat down and stuck the USB drive into my computer and began copying all the original files I had handed to Mark — the ones that were showing the negative returns, the ones that he demanded be altered. Bottom line was the company was in major trouble and this pending merger would be the only thing to save it, so it had everyone in a tizzy.

I had put in a ton of overtime hours in the last few weeks, which I already knew I wouldn't get paid for, just like all the other overtime hours. I seriously couldn't wait to get out of here.

I sipped on my coffee and then hit the print button, printing out all the original files I had done as well. I didn't want to solely rely on a digital copy.

My cell phone rang, and a smile came to my lips when I saw Don's name on the screen. "Hey, babe," I answered.

"You sure you are going to be on that flight?"

"Yes, why wouldn't I be? I'm just tying up a few things here at the office, and as soon as I am done, I'm running to grab my bags and getting on that plane. I'll see you at the airport at ten."

"Yeah, uh huh. You're sure it won't be like the last time? I sit waiting for you and you call me fifteen minutes after your flight was supposed to land and profusely apologize?"

"Don, I said I would be there."

"Yeah sure. I'll believe it when I see you step through those doors."

"Babe, seriously, I will be there. Everything is packed."

"Sure, yep, just like last time right," he barked.

"Don that was different, and you know it. It was a damn emergency."

"Yeah, and what about the time before that?"

"Don, I'll be there. I've got to go and finish so I'm not late. I'll see you at our usual meeting spot."

"Yep." He was gone before I had a chance to say good-bye.

I hung up my phone. That call had struck a nerve, but I didn't have time to think about it. I knew that once we were together, everything would be fine. I just wanted to get what I needed printed and copied before I left. I turned my attention back to the file and began printing off my payroll reports when Mark came striding into my office.

"So, Mia, about this vacation."

"What about it?"

"You aren't really leaving, are you? I mean I could really use your help here this week."

I couldn't believe what I was hearing. "I'm leaving in a few minutes, Mark."

He chuckled as he looked around my office. "I really thought you were kidding when you handed me the notif- ication of vacation. Unfortunately, I'm afraid that I need you to do some work for me, either here or while you are away."

"No way. Absolutely not." I ignored the fact that he was standing there in front of me.

"I just need a couple of hours of your time this week- end, and perhaps five- or ten-hours next week."

"Mark do I really need to remind you that I haven't had a vacation in fifteen years. I have two thousand and twenty-six-point-seven hours in my vacation bank. That is like a full year of time I could take off and you would have to pay me. Also, did you know that I have somewhere in the ballpark of almost thirty-five hundred hours of over- time that hasn't been paid out, since you stopped paying me my overtime three years ago?"

"Yeah, so what of it."

"What of it? It's illegal, Mark. It would take one phone

call to a lawyer, just one." I looked at him as if he were completely stupid.

He ignored everything I had said as if I hadn't even spoken. "Monday morning. I'll see you at eight. I will email you the list of what I need you to do this weekend, and I want to go over a bunch of things before the meetings with the lawyers in a few weeks. Just so we are on the same page."

"Yeah, right, Monday. Uh huh. I won't be here, Mark."

"I know you, Mia. You'll be here before I am. We've gone over this so many times. I will see you then." He left my office and carried on down the hall, whistling as he went.

I had created this, by always being so accommodating, always doing everything that he had asked. I had canceled plans with friends, family dinners, I had even gone into work the afternoon of my mother's funeral, all because I had been too stupid to stand up for myself. Now Mark was asking me to put my integrity on the line by fudging reports just so this merger would go through. All of his demands had finally pushed me over the edge, and I'd had enough.

I drank down the remainder of my coffee and pulled the reports from the printer, shoving them into my briefcase.

I wasted no time. I reached into my drawer and gathered my paystubs from the past year and shoved them into my bag, along with the USB from my computer. I wanted to make sure there was nothing left for the temp that was coming in to fill my spot. If there even was a temp, which there more than likely wasn't, since Mark hadn't even taken me seriously.

I glanced at the clock. It was almost 6:00 p.m. I would have just enough time to get home, drop my stuff off, and be on my way.

I got up from my desk and looked around my office, my second home, and smiled. I had everything I needed in case this backfired on me. I shut the lights off and was on my way to a week of freedom and the hope of a future husband.

Chapter Four

Mia

I had gotten off the plane and made my way over to our usual meeting place, just underneath the large bagel sign in the middle of the airport. I dropped my bags on the ground and looked through all of the people to see if I could spot Don. I didn't see him yet, and I glanced at my watch. We had agreed to meet at 10:00 sharp, and it was already 10:30. My plane had been a bit delayed, but he would have been able to see that. Perhaps he had run to the washroom.

I took a seat on a nearby bench and pulled out my phone to text him. I waited patiently for the phone to boot up, and once it had, I noticed I had a voice mail waiting for me. I already had a good guess who it was from, but I decided to listen to it anyway.

Only it wasn't Mark. My pulse pounded wildly in my ears as I listened to the message. It was Don. He wasn't coming. He was breaking up with me! My pulse hammered wildly in my ears.

"A fucking voice mail! Unbelievable!" I gritted under my breath, shutting my phone off and throwing it into my purse. "I flew halfway across the country to have him break up with me through a fucking voice mail. He could have saved me the trouble," I said out loud as I sat bouncing my foot impatiently.

A lady turned my way and smirked. I could tell she was trying not to laugh at my outburst.

My first vacation in fifteen years, and this was how it was going to start. I should have known from the signs that were presented to me earlier today that this whole thing was a bad idea. This upcoming merger had stressed me out so bad, and the fact that my boss was an inconsiderate prick who demanded more and more all the time had burned me completely out, and now this.

I had started to notice the burnout a few weeks ago when I couldn't get up out of bed on a Monday morning to go to our usual business meeting. I had been having trouble concentrating as well. Don had been my rock throughout most of it, trying to be supportive, but then he started expressing that he was beginning to feel ignored.

I tried to pretend that what he was saying wasn't true, but every time we had been together over the last few months, I had spent almost all my time working and ignoring him. I had hoped we had fixed our relationship enough; however, I guess we hadn't. I thought he would be getting down on bended knee professing his love for me sometime over the next week, but instead I sat here alone, feeling foolish. I probably would have been better off if I had just gone to the Dominican alone. Just one more mistake to add to my ever-growing list, and I had TexCorp to thank for that.

I dragged my bags behind me to the closest ladies room. Once inside, I slammed the stall door closed and leaned up against the cold brick wall. I took a couple of deep breaths and pulled out my phone. In those few breaths I decided that Don should tell me himself, not be a coward through a voice mail.

I dialed his number, expecting him to answer, but three rings later, his voice mail picked up. I hung up and pressed redial a couple more times, both yielding the same response.

"Okay so you don't want to answer. That figures. So I'll text instead," I mumbled to myself.

ME: I'm here, waiting at our normal meeting spot, under the bagel sign in case you've forgotten. Are you stuck in traffic?

I quickly used the facilities and had just finished

drying my hands when my phone buzzed in my pocket. I pulled my phone out and looked down at the screen.

DON: Nope, check your voice mail

My stomach sank. What a bastard. I dragged my suitcase behind me and went to sit down near the gate I would be flying out of. I had hours to wait for my connecting flight. We had planned it that way so we could spend a little time having a few drinks and dinner prior to taking off.

I shut my phone off and threw it in my purse. "I won't be needing you, that is for sure," I mumbled and sat back against the chair. The tension in my shoulders was incredible, and now I couldn't wait to hit that beach. I debated grabbing a room at a nearby hotel for the six-hour wait, that way I could get some sleep, but decided against it.

"What to do for six hours?" I questioned as I looked around, and then I saw it—Take me Away Bar and Grill.

I studied the sign. A gin and tonic would be great right about now, but like always, I decided against enjoying myself and pulled my book from my bag. Besides, I didn't want to get drunk before I flew.

I opened my book to the last chapter I had read and tried to ignore the craving for a cold beverage. Minutes later, I shoved my book back into my bag and shrugged my shoulders. "Fuck it, you're on vacation. You deserve a fucking drink," I said to myself, then grabbed my bags and headed over to the little bar.

As I entered, I looked around for an empty table. The place was busy, couples and families sitting, eating, laughing away. I had no one to sit and laugh away with, so I looked around for an empty seat. I finally spotted one at the bar and wandered over. I sat down and the bartender immediately took my order.

Within minutes, I took my first sip of the perfectly mixed gin and tonic, that first mouthful going down as smooth and as easy as water.

I fished around in my bag for my phone and head-phones, finally pulling them out and untangling the messed-up cord. I was going to sit here, drink my drinks, and listen to some music, maybe do a crossword or play a game on my phone, something, anything to help take away the fact that I was indeed sitting here alone, until I had to go.

I had powered up my phone and was just about to plug my earphones in when my phone rang. I frowned. Perhaps Don had realized he had made a mistake and changed his mind. Perhaps he was waiting for me.

"Hello," I answered.

"Mia," Mark's voice poured over the phone, causing me to roll my eyes, "about those reports. You missed one of them, my dear. Can you bring it in with you on Monday please?"

Of course, I had missed one. He would always find a reason to keep me where he wanted me.

"I told you, I won't be there Monday. I'm on vacation."

"Yeah sure, sure." He laughed.

That was it, I couldn't take it anymore, and just like that, I snapped.

Chapter Five

Bryce

"I'm not a greedy bastard, Chase. I am one of the most giving people there is. Alyssa, she doesn't see it that way," I mumbled into the phone as the cab drove up the hill toward the airport. "It really bothers me that she thinks of me that way, you know." I looked out the window, watching the snow start to fall.

"She's just pissed off that you won't let her stay in the condo anymore," Chase mumbled into the phone.

I was sure he was tired of listening to my whiny antics by now. I had decided to end my two weeks off a little bit early. Well, a lot early. A full week early. I had been inundated with calls from clients, and frankly, I was bored being here alone.

Alyssa normally came with me to the lake house. She would go off shopping or to the spa, and I would work, and then we would meet up in town and go for dinner. Some days we would both head up to one of the ski resorts and spend the day. Scratch that, she would take advantage of what I had to offer and end up calling me a greedy bastard in the end.

"You're better off, bro. Believe me."

I rested my head against the headrest, listening to the radio playing, the song making me think of Alyssa and the night we had broken up. She had called me a greedy bastard and made her way out the front door to her mother's because she hadn't gotten her way. That had been my breaking point.

I had given her every single thing she had ever wanted, no matter the cost. I knew my brothers thought I was crazy, but I was in love with her and I wanted her to be happy. Of course, my brothers had expressed their concerns many times, telling me how one-sided they felt the relationship was. The last family dinner we had together, Autumn, Hunter's wife, had even made a comment to Alyssa about the fact that she didn't seem to want to be there. Of course, then Hope jumped on her as well, resulting in a huge argument between all three women that ended when Alyssa stormed out of the house and waited in the car for me. It had been a disaster, and after that, she didn't bother coming to family dinners anymore, and every time I went, she felt the need to express her displeasure.

"Deep down I know you are right, Chase. Guess it's just a little hard for me to believe right now."

Alyssa was missing me. I had heard from her three times today alone, each call getting a little more desperate as the night went on. Finally, she admitted she had made a mistake and wanted me back, that she couldn't make it on her own. I didn't bother calling her back. Instead, I called my brother.

"I can't forgive her, Chase. Not knowing what she really thinks of me. I gave her three years, man."

"Forgive her? There is no way you should forgive her. She fucked another man in your bed. Besides, don't forget, you were treated like shit for those three years. So grow a pair and tell her to fuck off."

I laughed into the phone. This was my brother!

"I'll make someone happy one day, won't I, Chase?" I asked, interrupting whatever it was my brother was droning on about.

"Yes, of course you will. She isn't the last woman on earth, Bryce. Now stop sounding like a big pussy and reattach your dick. Do you think you are ready to return to work, because I seriously don't think you are ready to come back yet."

"Chase, I am fine. Seriously, there is so much work to do, so I am coming back. I just arrived at the airport."

"Well you best have a better handle on things. I'm not going to argue. I am drowning with this merger and could use you to go over the reports, but I know Carter and Hunter were pissed with you. If you don't feel you can come back yet, you best stay there."

"I'm good, honestly. I will be there and help you get everything in order. Listen, I got to run. Just arrived at my drop-off."

"All right. Talk to you later, bro. Safe flight."

"Thanks, see you soon."

Minutes later, I had paid my cab driver and found myself fighting my way through the crowds of people in the airport. I had come early. The lines were crazy long, so I wandered over to the window and watched the snow continuing to fall. As the flakes danced down to the ground, I wondered if perhaps I wasn't being ridiculous and probably should have had the taxi just turn around and return to the lake house. If this storm that they were promising started before my flight left, I'd have wasted my time.

Chase was right, I didn't need to be back in the city for another week, and to be honest, I truly didn't feel as if I were ready to go back. Instead the stubborn streak in me had insisted I get to the airport and head back home to the office and my new life. However, the ground was now covered with snow, getting deeper by the second. I looked up to see if my flight was still on time, and of course, it had been delayed and now wasn't scheduled to leave for another eight hours.

I wasn't going to waste my time worrying about it. I made my way over to the 'Take me Away' bar, deciding to drown my sorrows in a few drinks before my flight took off. I stepped up to the bar, signaling to the bartender, who held up his finger to let me know he would be with me in a minute.

I relaxed, glancing around the bar at all its patrons... and that was when I saw her. Mia, my best friend's little sister, was sitting on the opposite side of the bar on the phone, looking frustrated as hell.

I had to do a double take to make sure it was her, before I casually made my way over to an open stool beside her and took a seat. She hadn't noticed me yet. She was still talking with someone on the phone, determination, anger, and irritation lining her voice as she spoke.

She certainly hadn't changed, from what I remembered. Brown hair, cute button nose, still sexy as hell when she was angry. I listened to what she was saying, something about it being fifteen years and vacation and "I'm not working on that right now." Whatever it was, it didn't sound very good, and she certainly didn't look happy.

She stopped speaking, listened for half a minute more, and then hung up, slamming her phone onto the bar so hard I was afraid it may shatter. She picked up her drink and mumbled, "What an asshole," before almost emptying her glass.

"What will you have to drink, sir?" the bartender asked, pulling a clean glass from the stack.

"Double scotch on the rocks please, and another one for the lady please." I nodded toward Mia and handed the bartender my credit card. "Just start a tab please." I was going to be here for a while.

"Listen, asshole, there is no need to buy me a drink. I am perfectly capable of getting my own," Mia barked back.

"Mia, is that any way to treat an old friend?" I practically whispered in her ear.

Those big, chocolate-brown eyes of hers landed on mine. She blinked hard as she looked at me, a smile forming on her perfectly bowed lips. "Bryce? Is it really you?" she asked, her soft voice barely heard over the loud crowd. Her eyes swept over my body, taking in my large, muscular frame.

"Yes, Mia, it's me."

She was as beautiful as she had been all those years ago. Her long, soft, dark hair was pulled back in its signature ponytail, just like I remembered.

"It's so good to see you." She smiled, reaching up to give me a hug.

"You too." I wrapped my arms around her and pulled her close, breathing in her scent. "Is it okay if this asshole buys you a drink now?" I chuckled.

"My God, I am so sorry about that." She buried her face in her hands to hide her embarrassment.

"It's all right. No offense. How's that idiot brother of yours?"

Grant had been my best friend growing up. Of course, after college we went our separate ways—me to law school, him to medical school, and now we only saw and spoke to one another online.

"He's doing well. He's up for promotion at his hospital. Him and June just had their second baby as well." She smiled.

Second baby. Here I was still single, having stupid arguments and ending serious relationships with the women I dated, and my best friend was a father.

"Wow! That is great. I'm so happy for him. So what are you doing here and where you headed?" I asked, looking down at the luggage that sat in between her feet and the bar.

"Dominican." She picked up her drink and drank the rest just in time for the fresh ones to arrive.

"Visiting our old stomping grounds, I see. Although it

was much safer when we went. Now people only go there to get murdered." We both laughed.

I had often vacationed with Grant and his family growing up. We had spent two winters in the Dominican chasing girls and having fun. Well, he spent the time chasing girls; I spent my time dreaming of his sister.

She rolled her eyes at me and let out a little laugh. "I suppose I would have been. Figured it would be nice to go back to a familiar place."

"So where are you living now?"

"Oh, I still live just outside of Kings Cove Harbor. I never ventured very far."

I felt my heart race a little. She still lived near me. What a small world it was.

"Small world. I didn't travel far either. I work in the city still. So how did you end up in Vermont, if you are going to Dominican?" I questioned. They didn't normally re-route planes going to the Dominican here.

"Ugh, don't ask. As Grant would put it, it's just another one of my many stupid, stupid mistakes."

I let out a laugh. "That doesn't sound very good."

"Ugh, just my life lately. What about you? What are you doing here?"

I could tell she was frustrated, not just by the tone of her voice and body language but by the way she was fidgeting. Mia only ever used to fidget when she was agitated.

"I'm on my way back home. I came up to my lake house here for a little rest and relaxation." I placed my arm on the back of her chair.

"Nice. Well, I hope at least one of us had a good vacation."

She blinked hard and turned her face from me for a second, and that was when I saw one lone little tear slide down her cheek. I frowned.

"I'm sorry," she mumbled, quickly wiping her cheek. "I guess I am a little more upset than I first thought."

When we were younger, I had hated seeing her upset and always strove to make sure she never felt that way for any reason whenever she was around me, and tonight wasn't going to be any different.

"That's it, no tears!" I said, slapping the bar counter. Mia looked at me. "Tears are only going to call for many, many more drinks!" I signaled to the bartender for another round as Mia began to laugh. "And food," I said, reaching for a menu and handing it to her.

An hour later, it was just like old times again. We had caught up, and we sat with drinks in hand, the plate of fully loaded nachos gone, only a few crumbs left.

"That was so good," Mia said, relaxing back against her seat.

"That it was. Looks like you need another drink there." I signaled to her empty glass, then to the bartender for two more.

"I don't know. This is more than I've had to drink in a long time." She giggled.

I glanced up to the TV above our table and saw the current weather report. "Shit, that doesn't look very good." I tapped Mia's shoulder to get her to look at the TV. Snow had pretty much blanketed the area. The city was closing roads, and flight cancelations were now in progress.

"Well, that is just fantastic. Tops off a completely shitty day with yet another complication," she said as she threw her napkin down on the empty plate. "Now what?" She got up from her chair and began rustling through her purse.

"Calm down, Mia. We don't know for a fact that our planes are the ones that are canceled." She ignored me, continuing to search her purse. "What are you looking for?"

"My credit card. I need to pay my bill and get out there before—"

Before she could even finish what she was going to say, a voice came over the loudspeaker, quieting the whole restaurant.

"Unfortunately, due to extreme weather, all outbound and inbound flights have been canceled. I repeat, all flights currently reporting as delayed and on time have now been canceled."

That announcement stopped her in her tracks, and she sat back down on her chair looking defeated.

"Now what am I going to do?"

"Mia, it's not that big of a deal. We just come up with a Plan B," I announced, swirling my scotch and taking a drink.

She smirked. "It's no big deal? I pretty much had to sell a kidney to get my boss to approve this time off. Besides, I don't have a Plan B. I barely had a Plan A, and we can already see how that turned out."

"Well how about we come up with a Plan B together and we will go from there. If that one fails, then we come up with another one. Where is your sense of adventure? In case you've forgotten, my plans were always fun. You can't deny that."

I reached for the food menu and wiggled my eyebrows. "But first we need dessert. All good plans are derived over something sinfully sweet. Isn't that what you always said?"

I caught a glimpse of a smile, and together we looked over the menu and settled on a slice of cheesecake. I went with chocolate and she went with cherry and another round of drinks to wash it down.

Once the cheesecake was placed in front of us, she didn't hesitate. She sunk her fork in and then took a sip of her drink and let out a breath. I watched as she took another forkful and closed her eyes as she savored the rich flavor.

"So, tell me what Plan A was."

"If you really want to know, I came here to meet my boyfriend of five years. We'd been planning this trip for the last six months. I was pretty sure at the time we booked he was going to propose."

I looked around in a frantic search.

"Bryce, what is it?" she asked.

"Don't tell me I am sitting in his seat, hitting on his girl?"

She let out a laugh. "He's not here. As soon as the trip was booked, we started having...issues. He claimed that I don't try hard enough in our relationship, and that work takes a ton of my attention. I won't lie, it does take a ton of my attention, but never all of it. Anyways, he isn't here because that no-good son of a bitch broke up with me while I was flying here."

"He broke up with you after telling you that you don't try hard enough?"

"He did! Through a damn voice mail of all things."

"Through a voice mail? So, he blames you for all the trouble and then he does that. I'm sorry, Mia, but he sounds like a dick. I'd say you at least deserve a better breakup than that. I'd at least have the heart to call you before you traveled all the way here."

She let out a laugh. "Thanks, but honestly, it really

doesn't surprise me. Somehow, deep down, I figured he would end up being like that. Honestly, I'm not really all that torn up about it either. Funny thing is, since that voice mail, I feel as if a thousand-pound weight has been lifted off me."

I cleared my throat and took a sip of my drink. I certainly wasn't one to be giving relationship advice after everything I had gone through. I did, however, know how she felt because I had felt the same way after Alyssa walked out the door. I wasn't upset at the loss of her, more the idea of what she thought of me. I looked at Mia. She looked exhausted.

"All right! Well we can't stay here forever, so what did you want to do for Plan B? Any ideas?" she mumbled, swirling her fork around her plate, picking up little bits of cheesecake.

"Well, we can always head to my lake house. It's only ten minutes or so from here. It's got everything we need: a fireplace, hot tub, food, comfort."

She looked at me, a hint of playfulness in her eyes. "Really?"

"Yep. We can stay the week if you want. Let the storm pass over."

"That sort of sounds wonderful. Better than a beach vacation, to be honest."

That was the Mia I remembered. Even though she liked the beach, she always used to be more about comfort, and apparently, she hadn't changed. "All right, let me take care of the tab, and then we'll grab a cab."

"No, Bryce, really, I insist, let me."

"Mia, I'll take care of it," I said, placing my hand over hers to stop her from digging any farther into her purse. She turned those large brown eyes on me. I had expected her to argue, but she stopped and smiled.

I pulled my hand from hers and stood up from my seat. "Get your stuff together. I will be right back," I said winking.

I tapped my card on the debit machine and stepped off to the side to wait for the receipt. I looked over at Mia while I waited. She was your typical girl next door. Down to earth, no nonsense, attractive, and one girl I had always wanted but never had. Grant had told me the first time he brought me to his house when we were fifteen that his sister was off-limits. When I saw her, I instantly knew why. Of course, I did what most best friends would do—I kept my hands to myself and pined over her for a few years.

After we all parted ways, time separated us. I went on, and over the years, we lost touch, until I had forgotten about her completely...or I thought I had. However, the instant she appeared tonight it was like I had been transported back in time.

I watched as she pushed her dark hair behind her ear and licked her lips as she typed out something on her phone then shoved it back into her purse. I studied her closer. She looked tired and stressed, and I wondered when the last time was that she had any fun. It was that moment that I decided I was going to show her a fun, carefree week at my lake house. I had to, because judging from my body's response to touching her hand, I would be in trouble if anything else happened.

Chapter Six

Mia

Bryce stepped out from the curb and waved his hand in the air, signaling the next cab over. The car pulled up and the driver got out. "You again?" He chuckled.

Bryce started to laugh. "Yep, me again. Should have stayed at the lake house I guess."

"Going back, I take it." The man laughed as he came around and grabbed our bags.

Bryce opened the back door for me to get in the cab and slid in beside me. I sat back against the seat and watched out the window as we began the drive toward Bryce's lake house, the heat from the seats sinking into my body quickly relaxing me. It had been such a long day, and with all the stress, I had been put into a state of fight or flight, something I had long ago promised myself I would never get into again.

I closed my eyes, the smell of Bryce's cologne invading my senses. It was musky and manly and smelled so good I just wanted to bury my face in his neck.

"Would you both like to listen to some music?" the driver asked.

"Yes please," Bryce answered, and soon the cabin of the vehicle was filled with soft music. Within minutes, the song had changed on the radio to one that I remembered from my teen years. It instantly reminded me of a memory I hadn't thought of in a long while: the night of Mary McGuire's party.

It was the last party of the summer. Grant and Bryce had both graduated two months earlier and were packed and ready to leave for their respective schools. The following week, they would be gone. My brother was supposed to have gone to the party alone, but when I found out Bryce was going to be there too, I begged him to taking me. I knew this would be one of the last times I would have to hang with Bryce, and that was the only reason I had wanted to go. I'd had a huge crush on him since my brother brought him home in the tenth grade. Bryce never looked at me in the way I had hoped he would, even though I had tried so hard to get his attention.

Over the years, he spent many overnights at our house, and I would parade around him in my short shorts and tiny tank tops, praying for a glance, a look, anything. I would conveniently put myself beside him when he and my brother were watching a movie or beg to go to the theater with them, but Bryce never gave me a hint that he was remotely interested in me. In fact, he rarely if ever even noticed me.

During the summer before graduation, Grant, Bryce, and Chase did nothing but hang out around our pool. I had quickly gone from a one-piece suit that summer to a two-piece, and I would lie around and sun myself, reading books or magazines, while the boys played in the water.

At first, I received no attention, and just when I was about to give up, I started to notice Bryce watching me when no one was looking, his eyes skimming over my body.

The past school year, Bryce's interest continued. He would occasionally bump into me in the hallway between classes and sit and study with me during his spare in the library, claiming that none of his friends had a spare at the same time. Then, about halfway through the school year, Grant and Bryce had some sort of falling out, and he didn't come around to the house often. Almost instantly, he stopped sitting with me during spare. They had just started hanging out again at the end of summer, and once again he was back to ignoring me.

Grant and I had arrived a little after 9:00 p.m. The party was already in full force. "Really, Mia, I don't know why you even want to be here. You don't know anyone!" he said as he walked in front of me.

"That's not true. A few of my friends are here. I'll be fine. Just go and find your friends," I said, pushing him away.

Just like I wanted, Grant went off to find the boys, and I went to get a drink, quickly losing sight of my brother in the sea of people.

I wandered aimlessly for a couple of hours, looking for anyone I may know, getting new drinks along the way, until I finally spotted Bryce heading up the stairs. With my heart in my throat, I fought my way through the people, careful not to trip as I made my way upstairs.

I planned to make Bryce mine once and for all tonight. After all, I had seen the way he had looked at me.

As soon as I got up there, I noticed that most of the bedroom doors were shut. Lots of people lined the hall-way, but Bryce was gone. I slowly opened each door in search of him.

The first door I opened, I interrupted a couple who were almost having sex. Behind the second door the couple were making out on the bed. I knew he had come up here, so I shut the door and continued my way down the hall. Finally, I got to one of the last bedroom doors. It was cracked open and the light beside the bed was on, so I peeked through and saw Bryce standing there with his eyes closed.

I swallowed hard and finally, after I got up the courage, I pushed the door open a little and was just about to say "There you are" when he stepped forward and grabbed two hands. He pulled the owner of those two hands close to him, and that was when my breath caught in my throat. He was holding my best friend.

She stepped toward Bryce, and their lips slowly met. My eyes burned as I stood there. I didn't know what to do, except watch as every dream I ever had of kissing him shattered right before my eyes. I was frozen to the spot, so I couldn't move, and that was when Bryce opened his eyes and saw me standing there in the doorway. The look in his eyes was forever burned into my memory. That was when Kate turned and saw me as well. She had shouted something to me about being sorry and to wait, but I tore myself from that spot and ran with tears burning in my eyes. Halfway down the stairs, I felt my stomach start to turn, and I was now not only fighting the tears but also trying to stop the contents of my stomach from spewing everywhere.

I ran down those stairs, bumping people and getting dirty looks as I went. I just needed to get away. I didn't want to hear Kate's excuses. She knew how I felt about Bryce. How dare she do that to me?

I continued fighting my way through the crowd until I

ran into someone's chest. I felt a firm hand grip my shoulders, stopping me. I blinked and looked up to see my brother standing there, and that was when the tears started to spill down my face.

"Mia, what happened?"

"Nothing, Grant. Just take me home please."

I ripped from his grip and bolted out the front door, running toward our parked the car. I pulled open the back door and crawled in, curled up into a ball, and waited for what felt like ever for my brother. He wasn't too far behind, and he drove me home, asking me repeatedly what had happened and whose ass he and his friends needed to kick. I never said a word, and I never said anything to him about that night, and I never mentioned Bryce again to anyone. I had never even thought about him...until now.

That night had absolutely gutted me, and now just thinking about it, I realized that I still held onto that anger. The months that followed that night had been spent with my face down in the pillow. I ended my friendship with Kate and shut myself away from everyone else. I couldn't have a friendship with someone who would betray me like that, and I just wanted to be left alone anyway.

Grant and Bryce went off to school, and I was left to heal my broken heart. It was for the best.

I was yanked from my memory when I felt the car come to a stop and felt a light tap on my thigh.

"Wake up. We're here."

I looked at Bryce, and then out the window, and saw a dark house sitting at the end of a walkway.

A blast of cold air flew into my face as Bryce pushed the car door open, snow swirling inside. I shivered, pulling my coat around me.

"Let's go." He held out his hand out for me to take.

I grabbed my purse and climbed out of the back of the car with his help. He dug into his pocket and pulled a crisp bill from his billfold and handed it to the driver, who had already placed our bags onto the sidewalk. I took hold of my things, and together we walked down the walkway toward the front door.

"Careful, don't slip."

"I'm not five. I'm all right."

"Don't yell at me. I remember how accident prone you are."

Just as those words fell from his mouth, I felt my foot slip on some ice. I screamed as I felt myself start to fall backward, but he dropped his bags and grabbed my arms before I went down.

"You all right there?" he asked, steadying me.

"Yeah, thanks," I said as I regained my balance.

Once we were up and inside the covered porch, Bryce pulled his keys from his pocket and quickly unlocked the door. "I turned the heat down before I left, so you may want to leave your jacket on until I get a fire built. It's gotten much colder since then," he said, reaching inside and turning on a light. "Come on in and make yourself at home." He ushered me inside and shut and locked the door behind us.

Leaving our bags in the entryway, we removed our shoes and stepped into the living room. In the darkness I could see that this room looked out over the lake, lights of the other houses off in the distance twinkling like stars against the water.

Within seconds, that view disappeared when Bryce turned the lights on, and I saw our reflection in the glass. Bryce stood behind me, watching me. A funny feeling came over me, and it flashed through my mind for one minute that this was how it should have been—us together.

"Give me a few minutes to get a fire going," he said, and I turned, taking in the room while he bent down and started setting the wood up for a fire.

The large windows spanned from the floor to the ceiling, and I imagined that in the morning I would have a clear view of the storm we had just driven through. Maybe it wasn't such a bad idea I had come here. By the looks of things, I wouldn't be going anywhere for days and would have been spending my time in a hotel room instead.

I turned around, taking in more of the room. It was

decorated in dark greens and beige. An over-sized couch sat in front of the fireplace holding many large cushions and a couple of large fleece blankets that looked inviting. Two over-sized armchairs also looked comfortable enough to curl up into. The gigantic fireplace was gorgeous, the face of it appearing to be natural stone, and the wooden mantle was lined with photographs.

"Are those your nieces?" I asked, pointing to the photographs over the fire as I walked over to get a closer look.

"Yep those three are Carter's, and the other two munchkins are Hunter's."

I could see signs of both of his brothers in their kids. Backing away, I noticed a large TV that hung over the fireplace. I could easily see myself sitting down with a glass of wine and watching my favorite shows.

Returning my attention to the fireplace, I sat down on the arm of the couch and watched Bryce. He was squatted down, assembling some kindling in the fireplace, the sleeves of his dress shirt rolled up to expose his muscular forearms. I could see the strength in his back now that he had removed his suit jacket, as he reached for a larger piece of wood.

"As soon as I am done here, I'll show you around the place, then we'll get comfortable and grab something to drink."

It was only a few more minutes before the fire was roaring away and the heat was pouring into the room.

"Come, let's take a look around. It's only a one-bedroom house, so you can take the bedroom, and I'll take the couch," he offered as I followed him down the hall.

He opened the door and behind it was the most luxurious bedroom I had ever seen. It was almost bigger than my house, and again beautifully decorated and furnished with a king-sized bed, large sitting area in front of the large window, and another large fireplace.

"The bathroom," he said, opening another door and flipping on a light.

I poked my head in and saw a large soaker tub that could easily hold two, if not three, people and a massive walk-in shower.

"Wow, this is beautiful. You own all this?"

"I do," he answered as he pushed the closet door open and began shoving clothes to the back. "In case you want to hang some things up, go ahead. I'm going to go and grab us some drinks from the kitchen. Make yourself at home." He walked to the dresser and pulled open a drawer, removing his T-shirt and sweatpants. "Do you need anything warm to wear?" he asked.

"No, I should be fine. I did bring a couple warm things."

He nodded. "Well if you need anything, help yourself." He took his clothes and left the room.

I walked over and sat on the edge of the bed, my body sinking down into the soft mattress. I sat there for a couple of seconds, and then I opened my bag and pulled out my lounge pants and T-shirt, changing into them quickly before making my way back to the front room. I sank into the couch, relaxing as I felt the heat from the fire.

"Gin and tonic for you, scotch on the rocks for me." Bryce held the glass in front of me, and I reached up and took it. He placed his glass down on the table and sat next to me, pulling the blankets off the back of the couch and spreading them over us.

Chapter Seven

Bryce

I relaxed back and took a sip of my scotch, the ice clinking against the glass. I was just about to ask Mia more about her ex when my phone started to vibrate in my pocket.

"Give me one minute," I said, and pulled my phone from my pocket and answered it. Instantly, I regretted it. I should have known better. It was too late for any of my brothers to call.

"Bryce, there you are." Alyssa's voice poured over the phone, and I closed my eyes and clenched my fists.

"What do you want?" I barked.

She was the absolute last person on the planet I wanted to talk to right now...or ever again, for that matter.

"Have you gotten a place yet or should I just leave your shit at your brother's?"

I rolled my eyes and pinched the bridge of my nose with my fingers. She was like an instant headache.

"Alyssa. What on earth are you talking about?"

"I've been packing your things. I just wondered where you wanted me to drop everything. I know you have been staying with Chase over the last few weeks, so I wanted to make sure that's where you wanted everything before I drop it off."

I didn't give her another second. "Have you gone mad? It's my place! It's my condo, as in I pay the mortgage and the bills. It's your shit that has to go, not mine," I gritted into the phone. "It's been five months. I took pity on your sorry ass and I gave you three. It's now been two more past that."

"Chase..." she whined, the sniffles starting. I was sure she was pouring fake tears at this point. "You try finding a place in this city. It's not as easy as it looks, you know. Can't I just pay you rent and stay here?"

"No, Alyssa, I don't need a roommate. Now get off your ass and find somewhere to live. At this point, I really don't care if you live in a cardboard box. I am finished. I am not finding, nor am I paying for, you to find a new place to live, and you aren't staying there. Just get your shit together and go."

I frowned, squeezing the bridge of my nose with my

thumb and forefinger. I was so glad to be done with her and couldn't wait for her to leave. I had no idea what I ever even saw in her to begin with.

"Bryce?" she mewed.

"What?" I gritted into the phone.

"What about my ticket to Paris?" she questioned, and then grew quiet.

I couldn't believe my ears. "What ticket?" I gritted.

"The one you promised me."

I dropped my head back and took in a breath. It was taking all I had not to lose my composure. "When on earth did I promise you a ticket to Paris?"

"Seven months ago. It's just, I was thinking. Perhaps I could leave my things here and head over to Paris for a while to, you know, heal and find myself."

I let out a deep, hearty laugh, and then I felt the anger emerge and my chest start to ache. My head was pounding. She seemed to have a way of doing that to me lately.

"Alyssa, you have one more week, not a second, minute, or day more. Go to Paris, Italy, Australia for all I care. It's not going to be on my fucking dime. Now, I've got to go."

I hung up the phone and squeezed my fists tight. The woman absolutely infuriated me. I stood there letting the anger seep from my body before turning back to face Mia.

Maybe this storm was for the best. Perhaps I did need another week before I went back to everything. After all,

I would have gotten home, found her still there, and been back in the exact same position I had been in when I had left. I knew my brothers would be happy I took the time. After all, they were the ones who had forced me here.

"Bryce, is everything all right?" I heard Mia's soft voice ask behind me, and then I felt her small hand on my shoulder.

Ignoring her question, I turned and grabbed her hand. "Come with me." I pulled her down the hall as she followed behind me, laughing. I raced to the kitchen and down the set of stairs that led into my wine cellar. "All right, pick a bottle, any bottle, but make it a good one."

She looked at me as if I were crazy, but then turned and looked at the wall full of wine, finally reaching up and pulling one out. She handed it to me, and I looked down at the label.

"This couldn't be more perfect!" I said, looking in her eyes. I knew she was questioning what the hell had gone on over the phone, but instead of asking she just smiled at me and went with it.

I pulled another bottle from the wall and tucked it under my arm. "For later." I winked at her.

Within an hour, we were halfway through the second bottle while watching the storm unfold on TV. Mia's foot was casually draped over my leg, just like old times.

"So, tell me, that call you had..."

"Yeah, that call. Let's just say that call is part—no, that call is the entire reason why I am here."

She bit her lip, her eyes growing sad as she took another sip of wine. I could tell the alcohol was getting to her now because her eyes were bloodshot, and her cheeks carried a rosy hue.

"Bad?" she asked.

"You could say that. It's been a very stressful few months, to say the least. I've been helping with this huge merger that Chase is working on. The case is a disaster. Our clients think the company is holding back or lying about some information."

"Ah Chase. How is he?"

"Good, crazy as ever." I laughed.

She let out a little laugh that went straight to my cock, just like it used to do when we were younger.

"Oh and then my ex—oh my wonderful ex—decided to tell me one night that I'm nothing but a greedy bastard, so I broke up with her." I paused for a moment. "Well, that's not true. She broke up with me." I smiled at her and watched as she brought the wine glass to her lips, a smirk settling on them.

"A greedy bastard eh? I'm surprised someone would think that of you." She looked away from me, then cleared her throat. I knew exactly what she was referring to.

"All right, well, maybe when I was younger, but age changes people." I winked.

"Well something must have set her off. What did your boneheaded self do this time?"

She knew me well. Well enough to remember almost every breakup I had had.

"She got pissed off one night when I choose work over her. But really it wasn't like that. A client needed help. It was important, and I had to cancel our date. It wasn't the first time, but I always tried to choose her over work, and when I couldn't, I always made it up to her. She always said she understood, but for whatever reason, this time was different.

You know she told me that money meant more to me than she did. How ridiculous is that? At the time, she meant everything to me. She didn't understand I was only doing that to keep her happy, to be able to do the things that we both wanted to do, and to be able to go on the trips that she wanted to go on. It all takes money.

"You know what else took money? That two-carat diamond engagement ring I had custom ordered, that I was planning to surprise her with on our trip to Venice. All I can say is, it was a good thing I never gave it to her. When I had returned a couple nights later, after that argument, I found her riding another man in my bed."

Mia let out a little whistle. Perhaps I had divulged too much about the whole thing. I wasn't upset anymore, so I couldn't blame that. I was just angry now, and I feared that maybe I wasn't enough for any woman.

"I'm sorry to hear that, Bryce. No one should have to deal with that."

"It's okay. I was dealing with everything fine, until she wouldn't leave and started making me feel bad for asking her to. Then things started falling apart at work, and, well, here I am. Carter and Hunter had been watching it unfold, and when they figured I couldn't cope anymore, Carter decided to send me on a forced vacation!"

"Maybe it's all for the better? The breakup, the vacation, everything. The universe works in mysterious ways." Mia placed her hand on mine and smiled at me, her eyes glassy from all the alcohol we had consumed.

"You're probably right; it would never have worked anyways. I shouldn't have been so stupid. The writing was on the wall months and months ago."

We both sat there taking a moment to watch more of the storm on the television. It was coming down harder than before, and I was glad that we had this safe place to be.

When the silence became too uncomfortable to me, I sat forward and cleared my throat. "I want to make a toast," I announced.

"Oh yeah, to what?" She giggled.

"Here's to breakups and canceled plans!"

We clinked our glasses together and drank back the remainder of the wine, Mia reaching for the bottle and topping us off.

I had stopped drinking an hour earlier, and now we were sitting watching an episode of *The Big Bang Theory* when I looked over at Mia. She was slouched down on the couch, almost asleep, the wine glass half-empty in her hand and almost falling to the floor.

I reached over and took the glass from her, placing it quietly on the table. I got up and sat next to her. "Mia?" I whispered. She didn't respond, so I placed my hand on her shoulder and rubbed her arm this time. "Mia?" I said a little louder.

"Hmmm?" she moaned, keeping her eyes closed.

"Come on, let's get you to bed." I put my arm around her back and sat her up.

"What? Where are we going?"

"To bed. Come on."

She grabbed hold of my arm, and once she was up, she leaned into me. I placed my arm around her to keep her steady, allowing her to rest herself up against me. I shut the TV off and slowly walked her down to the bedroom, occasionally stopping so she could regain her balance. "Are you trying to take advantage of me?" She giggled between hiccups.

"No, just helping you to bed." I had my arm fully around her waist guiding her into the bedroom. Once we were at the bedside, I pulled the blankets back and sat her down first before laying her down. I swung her legs up and placed them on the bed, pulling the covers over her.

"Don't go," she whimpered as she rolled onto her side and grabbed my hand. "Stay with me."

"Mia, you're dreaming. Get some rest. I'll be in the living room."

She didn't make another sound and eased the grip she had on my hand.

I was just about to the door when she called my name again. I stopped with my hand on the door handle.

"Bryce, please stay with me. I want you to kiss me, like you kissed her..."

Mia started to snore as I stood there looking over my shoulder at her.

"The universe works in mysterious ways, buttercup," I mumbled, repeating her words from earlier as I looked back at her.

I shut the hall light off and the overhead light in the bedroom and turned on the bedside light. I sat down and placed my head in my hands. There was no way she could have remembered that night. It had been a shitty end to the year that summer. I had finally confessed my feelings for Mia to her brother and asked for his permission to start seeing her, and he flipped on me and told me to do what was best for everyone and leave her alone.

I had done just that.

I stopped everything, including my friendship with Grant, only seeing him when we all went out as a group. We had all planned on going to that party that summer, and I had heard from Kate, Mia's best friend, that Mia was trying to convince Grant to bring her. I knew how persistent she could be, and so I showed up at the party. If all else failed, at least I would hang with the guys for the last time before I left for school.

I had arrived early and was a few beers in, when I was approached by another one of Mia's friends and told that Mia was waiting for me upstairs. I couldn't wait. I had seen Grant, so I knew she must be there.

I excused myself from the group and went in search of the girl I wanted so bad. I found my way up the stairs and wandered down the hall to the room I was told she would meet me in. When I walked in, the room was empty, but I heard her in the bathroom. She called out for me to close my eyes, so I did, and shortly after I felt her hands in mine, and then I felt her lips on mine, and when I opened my eyes, it was like the floor fell out from under me.

Mia was standing in the doorway, watching everything unfold before her eyes. I had kissed Kate, not Mia. I had been tricked. I could remember the look in Mia's eyes as she backed out of the doorway, running from me.

I had run after her, but when I saw her speaking with Grant, I decided I'd better let sleeping dogs lie. If she told him, I knew he would kill me.

I left the party shortly after Grant did to take Mia home. I had gone by their place the next day when no one was home. I wanted to talk to Mia and explain what had happened, but no one answered the door. I tried one more time before I left for school. I knew she was no longer speaking to Kate; Grant had told me they had had some falling out before he had left for school. Once again, there was no answer, and I had no choice but to head on my way out of town for school. It had really been a horrible way to end the summer, considering it could have turned out so different.

Mia let out a soft moan behind me and rolled onto her back. I let out a breath and pulled my shirt off over my head and threw it over on the chair. Leaving my house pants on, I kicked my feet up on the bed and lay back, placing both arms behind my head. I turned and looked at Mia, who was now sound asleep on her side, her hands placed under her head.

"I wished I had a chance to make up to you for that night," I whispered. "Perhaps this week will be my chance."

Chapter Eight

Mia

I woke with a start to the sound of a phone ringing somewhere in the distance, the noise drilling into my head, and then I felt someone shove me. I was cold and uncovered, so I reached for the blankets, ignoring the noise, praying it would go away. I tried pulling a handful of the blankets I held, but nothing moved. Then I felt an annoying tap against my back again. I rolled over and looked through squinted eyes. I could see an outline of a form lying next to me.

"Mia, answer your damn phone," a husky, dry voice called out.

I blinked again and wiped my eyes. Bryce was sprawled

out beside me. I quickly turned my head away, breathing hard. What the hell was he doing in bed beside me?

I took a second to compose myself and then peeked again, still ignoring the ringing phone. He lay there shirtless, one hand over his eyes, the other resting on his solid eight pack of abs. I glanced farther down to see his foot rested on top of my leg, and I could make out the outline of his semi-hard cock through his pajama pants. We were both clothed, which was a good thing, but what the hell had happened last night?

I bit my lip and closed my eyes, trying hard to remember. Gin and tonics at the airport, wine, wine, and way too much wine. The very last thing I remembered was turning the TV to an episode of *The Big Bang Theory*.

"Mia, hell, answer your cell phone, my head is pounding." Bryce murmured, pulling the pillow over his face.

I reached around in my purse until I finally found my cell phone. "Hello." I waited, but no one responded. "Hello?" I repeated, rubbing my tired, dry eyes. When no one answered me this time, I hung up and rolled onto my back, looking up at the ceiling. I rested my arm over my eyes, still worried about what had happened between us.

I felt the bed move and shifted my arm just enough to peek over at Bryce. He was sitting up on the edge of the bed, his back to me. The absence of clothing allowed me to see more of him. His back muscles flexed as he stretched. He stood up and turned to me, his low-slung house pants accentuating his abs and that deeply carved V I had always loved.

He cleared his throat, pulling me from my thoughts. I didn't need to wonder what it would be like to run my tongue across those abs. I could feel the heat rising to my cheeks. I really needed a distraction.

"Nothing happened, just so you know."

I felt a sense of relief and disappointment run through me at the same time, but to be honest, it would have been a shame to have spent a night with him and not remember it.

"You were really drunk, so I brought you in here and helped you to bed. I guess I must have dozed off. I'm going to hit the shower. We should get up and have some breakfast."

Lying on the bed, I watched after him as he wandered into the bathroom and shut the door behind him. I wished I was part of what was going on behind that closed door.

I opened my eyes and looked around the room. It was quiet and I could see light coming in through the sides of the drawn curtains. I must have fallen back asleep while Bryce was in the shower.

I glanced at the clock on the table. It was 11:00 a.m. I stretched and went to the window, pulling back the curtains to look out. The dark gray skies were still threatening snow after all that had fallen last night, but the snow-covered landscape was beautiful.

I dropped the curtain, shutting the brightness out, and wandered into the bathroom, wet a cloth, and ran it over my face. I stepped back into the room, debating getting dressed, but my aching body had other ideas, and since I was still tired, I went and crawled back into bed. I was just about asleep again when my cell phone rang.

I ran my hand over my face and reached out from under the covers to dig my hand into my bag. I wiped my eyes and looked at the screen. "Seriously?" I huffed. I dropped the phone onto the bed and let it go to voice mail. Tara should know better than to call me while I was on vacation.

I rolled onto my back, rested my arm on my forehead, and stared up at the ceiling. I had just closed my eyes when my phone vibrated.

"Why," I cried. "Why are you doing this to me, universe," I asked and grabbed for my phone again.

I had three text messages and four emails all from Tara. I swallowed hard and read the emails, finding that she had a whole list of reports that Mark needed for Monday morning.

I quickly messaged her back asking if it could wait. Then I reminded her that I was on my first vacation in fifteen years and threw my phone back down on the bed. Within seconds, I felt the phone vibrate on top of the blankets and one simple word appeared on the screen. According to Mark the answer was "no."

I could already feel the stress seeping back into my body at her response, but I tried to shake it off. He wasn't getting them.

Wandering into the bathroom, I quickly showered, brushed my teeth, then flung my hair up into a wet ponytail because, well, I could, and then I dressed in a loose-fitting pair of jeans and T-shirt. I was glad I had packed a couple of warm things to wear. Grabbing my gray sweatshirt and my laptop, I made my way to the kitchen. It never mattered how much I didn't want to do anything for work, they always won, even now, because I could already feel the guilt of not doing it pour in.

I smelled the freshly brewed coffee the minute I emerged from the bedroom and followed that aroma to the kitchen. I rounded the corner, expecting to find Bryce, but instead I found plates of food spread across the island in the center of the kitchen. There was a little of everything, most of it having gone cold now, but nothing a microwave couldn't fix. Eggs, bacon, fresh fruit, dry cereal, pancakes, and oatmeal, everything looked great.

"Well, good morning. As you can see, breakfast awaits. Help yourself to anything you want. You may need to warm some of it up in the microwave. Also, there is yogurt in the fridge in case you want any, and fresh coffee. Would you like a mug?" I heard Bryce's deep voice behind me.

I shook my head in a yes motion and slowly walked into the kitchen, placing my laptop on the counter. I sat down at the island, opened my computer, and logged in. Bryce set the cup of coffee beside me, looking between me and the laptop.

"Is there Wi-Fi here?" I asked, taking a sip of the hot coffee.

"There is. Here." He came around to stand behind me, wrapping his arms around me, and quickly typed in the password and hit save. "There are plates right here when you are ready." Without another word, he pushed off the counter and left the kitchen.

The smell of pancakes and bacon made my stomach growl. I normally didn't have time to eat breakfast, unless I grabbed it from the coffee shop around the corner from the office—when I wasn't running late. I quickly fixed myself a plate of fruit, bacon, and pancakes and set it beside me while I logged into my remote office.

I had just popped a piece of bacon into my mouth and started working on the first report when Bryce entered the kitchen wearing running shoes and low-slung workout shorts, a green towel slung over his strong bare shoulder.

I looked up from my computer, slowly chewing. The first thing I noticed was his clear blue eyes. They stood out against his deeply tanned skin. His defined chest held a light sheen of sweat, and as my eyes traveled lower, I swore I could see the outline of his cock.

He looked down at the mess of papers I had scattered all over the counter and back up to me. "What you got going on here?"

I quickly piled the papers and took a sip of my coffee. "Nothing."

"Doesn't look like nothing to me. Looks like you might be doing work?"

"Nope," I said, taking a drink of my coffee.

"You're on vacation! It's time to shut things down." He picked up the papers I'd just piled, taking a strawberry from my plate and popping it into his mouth while winking at me. "Am I going to have to take these away from you?" he teased.

I let out a breath and smiled. Those blue eyes peered into mine, and a sexy smile was plastered on his face.

"No, and I know I shouldn't be working. It's just they are relentless, you know?"

"I get it." He stuck his tongue out at me, and I let out a little giggle. "All right, you have thirty minutes, then you are going to put this away. Then you should join me for a workout."

I took the paper from his hand. "All right. Go work out. I'm going to finish my breakfast."

Bryce smiled. "I'll be in here. Just going to do my run first. I know you aren't much of a runner."

"I'll be along shortly." I smiled and let out a laugh. "But you should know I'm not much of anything when it comes to physical activity."

"Gee, Mia, that is a shame." He winked as he walked by me and tapped me under the chin. "Thirty minutes. I'll be waiting."

I felt a surge of heat as I inhaled his scent and watched his ass in those low-slung gym shorts walk away from me and into a room off the kitchen. I cleared my mind, continued eating, and started working away. I got up to refill my coffee when I noticed Bryce had left the door open just enough that I could see him as he ran on the treadmill.

I couldn't tear my eyes away from him. I leaned against the counter and stood there drinking my coffee, watching him. A half hour later, I had long forgotten about the reports I was supposed to be working on, when he turned and looked into the kitchen. I still stood in the exact same spot watching him. I had only moved to grab more fruit. He gave me a sexy smile before shutting the treadmill off and grabbed his towel to wipe the sweat from his forehead and chest. He walked back into the kitchen and leaned against the counter, popping a piece of cantaloupe into his mouth.

"Like what you see, do you?"

I felt the heat rise to my cheeks. How was I going to hide this? I mean, I had literally been standing here drooling into my cup of coffee while watching the man run. There was no hiding it, he had caught me. What the hell was wrong with me?

I said nothing. Instead I drank down the last of my coffee, rinsed the mug in the sink, and placed it into the dishwasher. When I turned, he stood there watching me, a look in his eyes that I had never seen before.

"I thought you were going to join me?"

"I was," I said, straightening myself up from leaning on the kitchen counter, avoiding eye contact with him.

"Well, how about this. Since you made me run for an hour and I am done with my workout, why don't we go out and sit in the hot tub?" He stood there with a sexy smirk on his face. I felt like all the air had been sucked out of the room at his proposition. "Don't try to hide it, Mia. You know the idea sounds good." He winked. "And I am pretty sure you brought a bathing suit, since you were going to be in sun and sand, so you're not getting out of it. It's time to relax." He shut my laptop down and stood, leaning against the counter, looking at me.

Did I want to join him in the hot tub? Hell yes, I did.

The room was getting warmer by the second as we stood there staring at one another. I could barely breathe, so instead of saying anything, I grabbed my laptop and papers and looked over my shoulder at him as I quickly left the kitchen, shaking my head as I went.

"I hope you are getting changed!" I heard him shout behind me. "I'll be out back."

"I am! Meet you out there," I yelled back as I wandered down the hall as fast as I could and opened the bedroom door. I dumped everything onto the desk in the corner and turned to look over my shoulder out into the hallway. I thought for a second and then went over to my suitcase, lifting it up onto the bed. Unzipping the bag, I reached inside, pulling out a little white bikini, and let out a breath. Why the hell hadn't I packed a one-piece?

I went into the bathroom and changed, then looked at myself in the mirror. I played with the ties on my bathing suit for a second, and then grabbed one of the black towels and wrapped it around my body. I looked back at my reflection in the mirror one more time, trying to gather some form of courage of being almost naked in front of Bryce, and then shut the light off. I grabbed my flip-flops from my bag and made my way out to the back of the house.

I looked out the door and saw Bryce was already seated in the steaming water. He was facing away from the house and looking out onto the lake. I slipped my feet into my sandals and let out a breath as I stepped out the back door, the cold instantly hitting my bare skin. I clutched my towel, shivering, and ran to the hot tub and was just about to stop when my foot slipped on a patch of ice. I dropped the towel as I went down, letting out a scream. "Bryce, help!" I landed on my back with a *thud*.

Bryce jumped up and looked down to the ground. "My God, Mia, are you all right?" He jumped out of the tub and came rushing to my side. "Did you hit your head, anything broken?" he asked, placing his hand under my head to check for bumps.

"No, I thin

k I'm okay." I reached for the towel and groaned as I tried to sit up.

"Don't move." He picked me up off the ground with ease and sat me on the edge of the hot tub. He took the towel from me and I slowly lowered myself into the hot water, embarrassment reeling through me.

"Get in. You're going to get cold." He set my towel on the stairs and then climbed back into the tub.

Once he was seated beside me, I began to laugh at how embarrassing that was.

"What's so funny?"

"I am just embarrassed is all, about the fall."

"Don't be. I remember how accident prone you are. Do you remember the time you went into the house to grab a drink for yourself and came back out to the pool and tripped over Grant's pants? You went headfirst into the pool, your drink flying, and when you hit the water, your bikini top flew off." He laughed.

"Oh God, don't remind me. I wanted to die when I noticed it had come off," I said, laughing at the memory, my hands covering my face.

"All my sixteen-year-old brain wanted was a little flash, but you covered everything up so tight it was impossible to see anything." He winked and reached over the side of the tub, grabbed a wine cooler, opened it, and handed it over to me. "Here you go!"

My face flamed with embarrassment, but I did my best to brush it off and took the cold bottle from his hand and took a sip. "What's this for?"

"We are celebrating our breakups today!"

"What do you mean, celebrating?"

"Let's be honest with ourselves. Obviously neither of us were meant to date these douches that we were involved with, and we are totally better off without them, so we are going to celebrate, baby!"

I let out a loud laugh. He was right!

"So, aside from this breakup, which was your worst?"

"Well, I guess it would have been when I was in my early twenties. I was out with my friends when a group of guys my friends knew showed up. I didn't know it at the time, but it was a fix-up. Anyways, I was introduced to the quiet guy in the back, Brenden. You could tell he was the bad boy of the group, you know what I mean. I was instantly attracted to him. We started seeing one another, but I really wanted to play it cool just so he didn't know how much I liked him. It became more of a push-pull type of relationship. One week he would want me, the next I would want him. Anyways, things finally got serious once we were done playing that game, and he moved in with me. We survived Christmas and Valentine's Day, and then things kind of crashed and burned."

"What happened?"

"I came home from work one afternoon, and a voice mail—no surprise there—was waiting on the machine for him. He had apparently been seeing a girl on the side and she called to let him know she was three months pregnant. I was so crushed, my heart broken, I packed up his things before he got home and left them down on the sidewalk for him." I drank down more of my cooler, looking over to Bryce.

"Wow, maybe you should get rid of voice mail. There seems to be a pattern here."

I let out a laugh.

"Honestly, I don't even know what to say to that," Bryce said, drinking back his beer.

"Well, what about you?" I asked. "What is your worst story?"

Bryce looked up from the bottle he was holding. With one look I could tell he had something on his mind that he was holding back for some reason. "It was this one, to be honest," he said, getting quiet again.

I looked over at Bryce and cleared my throat before downing the remainder of my cooler. "You know what this calls, for don't you?"

"No," he answered, pulling himself up out of the tub to sit on the edge.

"Meatballs!"

"Meatballs?"

"Yeah meatballs! Let's go make some. They are the perfect comfort food, trust me!"

Bryce watched as I climbed out of the tub and wrapped myself up in the towel, obstructing his view. "You coming?"

"All right, let's go make meatballs!"

<h1 style="text-align:center">Chapter Nine</h1>

Bryce

"You mix while I add ingredients," Mia said, opening the pantry door and pulling out a bunch of dry ingredients, while the ground beef defrosted in the microwave.

She stopped and went over everything she had pulled out, mentally remembering the ingredients, her face lighting up when she recalled the one she was missing.

"Did you want some wine before we start?" I questioned while grabbing the bowl and measuring cups she handed me.

"Um yeah...that is just a silly question. I'll grab the glasses."

The microwave beeped and she pulled the ground

beef out and dumped it into the bowl, while I went down and grabbed us two bottles of wine. I returned to the kitchen and opened and poured us our wine.

"When you're done, could you break up this ground beef? Do you have any oatmeal or breadcrumbs?" Mia asked while searching the cupboard.

"I can do that. Oatmeal is on the top shelf; breadcrumbs are in the green container," I answered as I dug my hand into the cold beef and began to break it up. I couldn't help but watch her bend and grab the breadcrumb container. She had the most perfect ass.

She set it on the counter and opened it, taking a couple of handfuls and dumping them into the bowl, along with an egg for me to mix. I dug my hands into the cold meat and watched as she carefully measured and added a bunch of spices into a separate bowl.

"Make sure you mix it all together really well, and then we will add in these spices. Where do you keep the baking sheets?"

"In the cupboard beside the stove."

Soon we were through with the first bottle of wine and onto the second when we began rolling meatballs and placing them one by one onto the pan while the oven was heating to the desired temperature.

"Just you wait, I'm telling you, these meatballs are the best comfort food in the world."

"Eat a lot of these do you?" I joked.

Mia stuck her tongue out at me before taking the tray and putting them in the oven.

"Now for more wine! You want to pick another bottle or shall I this time?"

"Go for it!" she said, and I walked over to the top of the stairs and turned to look back at Mia. She had already begun to clean up the kitchen. I hadn't realized it before, but I had really missed her and her brother in my life.

I watched as she danced around the kitchen, putting ingredients back where she had taken them from and placing things in the sink to quickly wash up and put away. I stood there for a few minutes continuing to watch her, wishing I could correct the lie that I had told her earlier. That the breakup I had just been through wasn't really the worst breakup. What was my worst breakup was the night she had seen me with her friend. That the worse part of it was having to say good-bye to her. However, I already knew there was no way that I could. So, pulling my gaze from her, I trudged down the stairs to pick our next bottle of wine.

While the meatballs cooked, we both showered and changed into some loungewear. As darkness fell, snow had started to fall again, and I had just built a roaring fire in the fireplace. I had soft music playing and two glasses of my favorite wine poured. I had just finished placing the bottle back into the chiller and dimming the lights when I saw Mia from the corner of my eye come into the room carrying a tray.

"Here they are!" she sang as she set the tray down, meatballs piled high on one plate and crackers and cheese on another.

I held out a glass of wine for her and she reached out and took it from me, looking around the room as realization came to her face.

"What is it?" I asked.

"Bryce, is this how you seduce women? I mean, look at it here. A beautiful lake house, hot tub, fire, dim lights, food and wine?" The light was dancing in her eyes as she looked at me.

I grinned. "No, the seducing part comes later—much, much later," I joked. "Just thought it would be nice to relax a little. Now let me taste these meatballs you rave about!"

She didn't hesitate. She grabbed one from the pile and brought it to my mouth.

"Be careful, it might be hot inside."

I took a bite, my teeth sinking into the soft inside. It was the best meatball I had ever tasted, and I closed my eyes as I chewed. When I opened my eyes, Mia was studying my face, a look in her eye I hadn't seen on her before.

The silence between us was becoming a little uncomfortable, so I took the remainder of the meatball that she held in her hand and put it to her perfect lips, watching as she parted them and took it from my hand. As soon as her teeth sank into the warm meat, she too closed her eyes.

She was fucking gorgeous.

I couldn't help myself. As soon as I knew she had swallowed, but before she opened her eyes, I leaned down and took her mouth with mine. She didn't move as I kissed her lips, her body stiffening at first, but I held her in my arms, and soon the plate of meatballs was forgotten, and she was a puddle in my arms.

We fell to the couch and curled up together, her in my arms as I continued the assault on her mouth, my tongue forcing her lips apart. I could already feel myself straining against my pants, and I gripped her ass while I kissed her deep. I pulled her closer to me so she could feel what she was doing to me, my mouth moving from hers down to her neck. I felt her place her hand between us, resting it on my chest, signaling me to give her a second.

As I pulled my lips away, I noticed her breathing was hard and erratic and she was having a hard time catching her breath. I gave her a couple of minutes, letting her calm down a bit before taking her hand in mine.

"Come with me," I said, sliding off the couch and helping her to stand.

Together we walked hand-in-hand down the hall toward the bedroom.

"Where are we going?" she asked innocently.

"You'll see. Just keep an open mind okay." I couldn't take it anymore. I wanted her naked, but at the same time, I didn't want to scare her away. I had spent half my teenage life thinking of her perfect pink lips wrapped around my cock as she looked up at me through that mane of messy, soft, thick brown beautiful hair. The more I thought of it, the more I could feel myself getting harder at the thought of her doing that to me.

I shut the bedroom door behind her. She stood there watching me as I wandered into the bathroom and turned on the shower. It didn't take long before the steam was rising over the shower door, the glass starting to fog up. I dropped my gear, glancing out the door to catch her watching me, and then I got into the shower, my heart speeding up at the thought that I might have taken things with her a little too far and that she may not join me. I knew she wanted me, I could see it in her eyes, but I was still worried.

I ran my hand over the length of my cock. If I couldn't get satisfaction out of burying myself inside her and listening to her moan, then I guess good old faithful would do.

I shut the shower door behind me, the steam now thick enough in the bathroom that I couldn't even see my own reflection in the mirror. I placed one hand on the wall to balance myself while the hot water ran over my body, and I slowly stroked my cock with the other. I was hard as a fucking rock, and it was such a shame to waste this, but it needed to be done.

I stroked myself another couple of times, relishing the sensation, but stopped when I thought I heard the bathroom door creak open. I gripped my cock, continuing to stroke it, when the shower door opened, letting in a rush of cool air, and a naked Mia stepped inside.

My heart nearly stopped as she shook her hair from the ponytail she had it in, her breasts on full display for me. Her eyes trailed down to the hand that was wrapped around my cock, a light flush on her cheeks as she bit her lip and shut the door behind her.

I let my eyes wash over her body, her perky breasts before me, her rosy pink buds calling to me, practically begging me to suck on them. I looked up and met her eyes. She looked a little unsure of herself, and for a second I was afraid she may just turn and run. She hid her eyes quickly and her cheeks turned a deeper shade of pink as her eyes wandered down my body, landing once again on my already hard cock.

"I don't even know what I am doing," she whispered, and once again, I was sure she was going to run if I didn't act fast.

I didn't give her words another thought. I reached out and wrapped my hands around her waist, pulling her against me and meeting her lips with a harsh, demanding kiss, my tongue exploring the inside of her mouth, while the hot water washed down overtop of us. I tore my lips from hers. "Just go with it. This week is about letting go, remember?"

I pushed her up against the wall of the shower and kissed her again, taking her hands and wrapping them around my waist. I ran my hands over her breasts gently, running the palms of my hands over her nipples. I cupped them in my hands, feeling the weight of them as they rested there. It was a matter of seconds before I rubbed the pads of my thumbs over her nipples again, and she sucked in air and let out a beautiful little moan that went straight to my cock.

I stifled her moan and kissed her lips again, while running my hands through her thick, soft hair. She placed her hands on my chest, stopping me. "What are we doing? What am I doing?" she mumbled between kisses.

She had always been a little uptight, I remembered that from years ago. "Shhh, just go with it," I whispered, taking her earlobe into my mouth. "Who would have thought I'd still want you after all this time? I've waited twelve years for you," I whispered, those words slipping out before I could stop them.

"Bryce?"

I kissed her hard and turned her around, pulling her back flush to my chest. I needed to distract her from what I had said. She wasn't supposed to know. I kissed her neck and ran my hand down between her legs, my fingers quickly sliding into her folds. She was already wet for me, and I groaned as my fingers slid over her, rubbing her clit in slow circles. She dropped her head back against my shoulder and sucked her lower lip between her teeth. "Feel good, baby?" I whispered in her ear.

She moaned her approval, so I kept going, my other hand reaching up and taking her nipple and rolling it between my fingers. When I felt her start to shake, I stopped, pulling my hand from between her legs.

She let out a small whimper. "Don't stop."

"I'm not, but there is no way I'm letting you come that way," I said, spinning her around to face me. Pushing her up against the wall of the shower, I kneeled before her. Holding her in place, I raised one of her legs over my shoulder and buried my face between her legs, sucking and licking her clit, while I buried two fingers inside of her.

Within minutes, her fingers were entwined in my hair and she was trying to stifle every sexy moan that came from her mouth, while her body was pressed against the wall of the shower.

A few deep pumps, and I began to feel her tighten around my fingers, I sucked her clit into my mouth and ran my tongue over her. Her legs began to shake, but I didn't stop. I kept going until she exploded in my mouth, her screams getting louder and louder.

Chapter Ten

Mia

I could feel Bryce holding onto me as I stood against the shower door, my eyes closed, my body shaking from the orgasm he had just given me. I could feel his breath against my lips and opened my eyes.

"You let go," he whispered, his lips meeting mine.

His kiss was exactly how I imagined it would be, and as hard as it normally was for me to let go, for some reason, with him, it was easy. If I were being honest with myself, it had felt good to lose control and not think about anything for a few minutes.

"Come on, let's go." Bryce shut the water off and opened the shower door. He grabbed a large black towel and wrapped it around me, then secured one around his waist.

My legs were still shaking as I took a step forward, so instead, Bryce picked up my sated body and carried me into his bedroom. The room was dark, and he lay me down gently on the bed, crawling in beside me.

"Your sheets are going to get all wet," I said, smiling up at him.

He bent down and met my lips. "Doesn't matter," he whispered, brushing strands of wet hair from my face. "Remember...letting go."

He tugged at my towel and unwrapped it from my body, his fingers grazing the soft skin of my tummy. "You are beautiful," he mumbled, placing little kisses along my collarbone.

I heard a loud grumble come from Bryce's stomach and began to laugh as he continued to trail kisses down my body. "Are you hungry?" I asked.

"A little," he said, placing another kiss on my lips. "Nothing you won't fix."

I traced his lips with my finger. "How about I go and get you something from the kitchen."

"No, it's okay." He kissed down my chest. He was just about to swirl his tongue around my nipple when his stomach gave another loud growl.

"No, let me grab you something," I insisted, sitting up and wrapping the towel around my body.

"Take my robe. I don't want you to get cold. It's hanging behind the bathroom door."

I grabbed the heavy terrycloth robe and wrapped it around me and made my way to the living room first to get the food we had left, and then I wandered to the kitchen. I quietly pulled out the plate of fresh fruit and searched the cupboards for another plate. My hands shook with every move. I couldn't believe what we had done. I was not a spontaneous person by any means, and I could feel panic setting in. I had dated Don for almost a year before falling into bed with him, and my relationships before that took two years. I had never just jumped into bed with someone before, let alone a friend. I couldn't figure out what made this different.

I took a deep breath, steadying my hand while I piled food onto the two plates I had just pulled out of the cupboard, when I heard a throat clearing behind me. I turned abruptly to find Bryce standing there leaning up against the doorframe in low-slung house pants, a sexy-ass smile plastered on his face as he watched me.

"I told you I was coming right back." I giggled and continued loading the plates.

"I was lonely," Bryce said, pushing off the wall and coming up behind me, wrapping his arms around my waist and kissing my neck.

I placed the two plates down onto the island and watched as he grabbed a strawberry from one. He bit into it, and then I felt him run the cold berry over my neck.

"What are you doing?"

"Having a snack," he whispered as his mouth met the trail of strawberry juice on my neck.

I couldn't help but close my eyes and just feel his lips trail over my skin. I could feel myself getting wet again and pulled out of his embrace. "You need to eat."

He pouted as I stepped away and pulled down two mugs from the cupboard. "Tea?" I asked, switching on the kettle.

"Please." He piled a few more meatballs and cheese onto his plate and sat on one of the stools that lined the island.

The roar of the kettle whistled behind me as I popped a strawberry into my mouth. I filled two mugs with hot water and placed one in front of Bryce.

"So, where do you practice?" I asked, munching on another strawberry. "You said you were still in Kings Cove."

"Yep. Once Hunter graduated, he and Carter opened up a small law firm. By the time I graduated, they had more on their plate than they could handle, so I joined them. Chase did as well, eventually. I am currently working towards making partner. We sort of each studied and specialized in different parts of law so that we could have our own fully functioning family law firm."

I walked around and sat down beside Bryce and ate a few more pieces of fruit, while he did the same.

"So you guys are still pretty close then."

"Very. Aside from working together every day, we have family dinners every week. A time to put work behind us and just spend quality time together. They also share this place with me. This was supposed to be Hunter and Autumn's vacation weeks, but they canceled. They are due to have their third baby any day now."

"That is great to hear. Congratulations to them. Actually, I never thought Hunter would ever get married. I remember Grant always idolizing him."

"Yeah, I remember. Hunter was always chasing tail."

"So were you," I muttered.

Bryce stopped, his hand halfway to his mouth. "What are you talking about? I never..."

"Please." I let out a laugh. "You were too. I used to..." I stopped before I let it all out. He couldn't know.

"You used to what?"

"Nothing, never mind."

"No, by all means, say it."

"I used to hear the rumors," I lied.

We both grew quiet. I couldn't believe I almost admitted that I was jealous of every girl he ever dated. There was no way I could let that slip, no way.

We both sat quietly munching away and sipping tea. Bryce glanced at me every now and again, meeting my eyes. "So, I don't have to worry about this voice mail heart-breaker showing up here and kicking my ass, do I?" he asked, studying my face.

"No." I laughed. "Seriously, we were never going to work out. I knew it, and he knew it. It just took us five years to figure it out, I guess."

"I see."

"What about you?"

"Did I know it wasn't going to work out between the two of you?" He chuckled.

I started to laugh. "No, do I have anything to worry about?"

He looked at me and smiled. "Why would you be worried?"

"Hey, if you give girls orgasms like that all the time, I just want to make sure she isn't going to come back and claim you." I could feel my cheeks heating. Claim was the wrong word. It sounded like I didn't want to lose him, when the truth was, I didn't have him, and I'd never had him. This was a week of letting go, nothing more, so I shook the thought from my head.

"She isn't coming back to claim me. She may think she could, but it's over for me. She gave up her right to me when she fell into bed with someone else and became a snarky bitch in the process."

The room got quiet as we both looked at one another.

"Have you had enough?" he asked, signaling to the plates of food that we had pretty much picked over.

"I'm good," I said, placing my hand on my full belly.

He busied himself cleaning up the dishes and condensing what was left over onto the same plates. As soon as the plates were covered and back in the fridge, Bryce looked at me, his blue eyes giving away his thoughts.

"What?"

"I want to show you something. Come with me." He held his hand out to me.

I placed my hand into his large, strong, warm hand and followed him out of the kitchen and down the hall. He stopped at the patio door and tied the robe I wore tight around me.

"Stay here for a minute. Just going to open the hot tub."

I watched him as he ran out, his arm and back muscles flexing as he opened the tub and then ran back to the door and took my hand. "I don't want you to fall again," he said as he carefully walked me over to the edge of the tub.

Without even thinking, I dropped the robe, exposing my naked body to him, and climbed in. He then ran back and shut the outside light off, so we were bathed in darkness with nothing but the stars twinkling above us.

"This is it isn't it? Now, after all we have been through, it's going to come to an end. You're going to drown me in the dark so that neighbors don't see." I giggled. "It's over."

Bryce let out a chuckle. "Not at all." He dropped his lounge pants and climbed into the tub, lying back in the reclining seat. "Come over here."

I moved from the seat I was sitting on and slid my body between his legs. He slipped his arm around me, and I leaned back against his chest.

"Just take a moment and look up."

I did as he asked, seeing thousands of twinkling stars lined the night sky. They looked like millions of diamonds on a black background.

"This is amazing," I whispered, seeing a shooting star travel across the sky.

"Yes, it is. Honestly, this is my favorite part about being up here, coming out here and looking at all this."

My body resting against his, he wrapped his arms around my waist and gently kissed my ear. I relaxed into his arms and studied the night sky with him.

"You see that?" he asked, pointing to a grouping of stars.

"Yes."

"That is the Gemini constellation, Castor and Pollux. And that one is Orion's Belt..."

"Where does this come from?" I asked, stopping him from what he was going to say next.

"What?"

"All this star talk?"

"As a kid I loved astronomy. I would sit with my telescope and study the sky for hours on end."

"Really? I don't remember you ever mentioning anything about that."

"My brothers used to make fun of me for it, and once I hit my teens, I realized how much of a geek I really was. Girls really didn't like that stuff anyways." He grew quiet, and I could tell he was a little uncomfortable sharing this stuff with me.

"You dated the wrong girls." Realizing what I had just said, I cleared my throat and waited for him to continue.

I could feel him looking at me, and I closed my eyes quickly, hoping that he'd just continue. "What is that one?" I asked, pointing in the direction, hoping to distract him.

I listened as he rattled off constellations and the stories behind them, reciting them as if he had written them himself. As I lay there, I couldn't help but feel things that I probably shouldn't be feeling. After a while, he went quiet and pulled me tighter into him.

I could feel something inside of me that I hadn't felt in a long time, if ever. As I closed my eyes and listened to the sound of his breathing, I thought about my future. I could actually see myself marrying this man. How someone could throw him away and he now be single was beyond me. Maybe the universe was trying to tell me something by stranding me in the airport and strategically placing him there as well, giving us a chance to meet again.

A little while later, I was standing on the deck, wrapped in Bryce's bathrobe, waiting for him to close the hot tub and go inside. It was late and we were both tired.

"All right, let's go," he whispered.

I took a step toward the house when he gripped my wrist from behind, stopping me from moving any farther. He pulled me tighter against him and we looked into one another's eyes. He said nothing; he just held my gaze. I was about to say something when he leaned down and took my mouth with his.

This kiss was different from the others we had shared today. It was slower, deeper, and contained a hint of emotion as opposed to the pure, lust-filled want the others had carried. My heart beat hard, as his lips meant mine, this kiss, his kiss taking my breath away.

Chapter Eleven

Mia

"Here's breakfast." Bryce placed a plate of waffles and fruit in front of me. Once we woke this morning, after an incredible night, we had just lounged in bed in one another's arms.

"This looks fantastic," I said, reaching for the syrup and pouring the sticky liquid over the fresh homemade waffles on my plate. Bryce sat down across from me and I handed him the syrup. He did the same.

"Okay, so, it has cleared up enough outside, and the roads are able to be traveled. How about we take a trip into town today? We can go to the market, visit some shops, have some lunch. What do you say?" he asked, digging his fork into the waffles.

"Sounds great. I just have an email to respond to before..."

Bryce looked up at me, his fork now halfway to his mouth. "No, Mia. No responsibilities. Vacation remember? Letting go of everything." He reached across the table and picked up my cell phone, pocketing it. "This will stay here today in the bedroom, along with mine. You can have it back when we get back. I'm on a mission to teach you how to have fun and let go," he said, winking at me.

"I have fun!" I exclaimed, rolling my eyes and laughing.

"When? Sitting in your pajamas at midnight doing reports? That's not fun, Mia. That is work. Now, last night that was fun." He winked at me.

He had a point. Aside from the last couple of days, I couldn't remember the last time I'd had a day without some part of work in it.

"Don't you ever just go out and have fun with friends?" he asked.

Somehow, over the years, the girls I hung out with had stopped asking me to join them. They would call, I would tell them I was too busy, and before I knew it, they just stopped calling. Those calls never came in anymore, and to be honest, I couldn't remember the last time I had spoken to any of them. "Not anymore," I mumbled.

"Mia, life is way too short, babe. You got to have fun,

so today, we are going to have fun! It will be like we're sixteen again."

I let out a laugh and dragged my fork around my plate while thinking of what he had said. Those fifteen years without a vacation went by in a blink. When Mom got sick, even though it felt as if time stood still, I think it went by even faster. Bryce was right.

"Okay, I won't argue. Let's eat and get ready."

We lounged around for the rest of the early morning, cleaning the kitchen after the mess of breakfast, watching a little TV, our legs entwined together as we cuddled under a blanket and competed against one another while watching *The Price is Right*. After that, we had showers and got dressed. The taxi had just arrived when I emerged from the bedroom, and soon we were in the back of the cab driving through the downtown area. I looked out the window to see the area was bustling with people.

"Sir, if you could just drop us in front of Lake Champlain Chocolates, please," Bryce asked.

"Sure, thing, sir."

"What is that?" I asked, taking in his handsome, strong features.

"I guess you will have to wait and see, but I will give you a hint: they have the best hot chocolate in the world."

Before we new it, the cab had pulled up in front of this cute, cozy little shop, and we both got out of the car.

My mouth began to water as soon as I stepped onto the sidewalk. I could already smell the chocolate.

I waited while Bryce paid the driver and looked around at the shops on the street. Bryce turned toward me and smiled.

"Can we go over to that store over there?" I asked, pointing to a cute little antique store across the street.

"Of course, anything you want, but first I am dying for some of this. Come on." He placed his hand at the small of my back and guided me through the door.

We stood in line, and I couldn't help but look at all the items in the display case. Everything looked so good.

"Okay, so you have to try those," Bryce said, pointing to one of the desserts in the display case. "We will get those to go, for later tonight."

"What is that?"

"Heaven!" he stated, smiling at me, while pulling me close and kissing my cheek.

After we had been served, we chose a quiet corner in the back of the little shop, away from all the people. I took a sip of the hot, thick chocolate and let it sit in my mouth, my taste buds exploding. It was the perfect blend of bitter and sweet.

"Good isn't it?" Bryce asked.

I nodded my head and took another sip, once again savoring the mouthful. We sat across from one another, a plate of chocolates between us. Bryce picked up one of the chocolates and held it out in front of me. "Open up."

I opened my mouth and he slid the chocolate inside. I bit down, and a burst of orange mixed with the bitterness of dark chocolate rushed into my mouth, and I closed my eyes to savor the taste.

"Well?"

"It's like an orgasm in my mouth," I muttered, savoring the sweetness.

He chuckled at my response.

"Okay, your turn," I said as I picked one up and held it out for him to try. He took it from my fingers and bit down. I watched his expression light up as he swallowed.

"My God, Mia, amazing choice. A mix of peppermint and chocolate, my favorite.

We sat there, each of us going back and forth, taking turns feeding one another, trying the chocolates. I had just swallowed the last bite of my chocolate when an older woman sat down next to our table.

"All right, only two more. Which do you want?" Bryce asked, bringing me back to our table.

I hesitated, looking back over at her. I could see the woman was watching us, a slight smile on her lips. I did my best to ignore her and picked one of the chocolates, Bryce taking the other one. At the exact same time, we popped them into our mouths, our eyes lighting up at the taste, and we both broke out into laughter.

"Raspberry!" we both exclaimed at the exact same time, continuing to laugh.

"Excuse me," a soft voice broke into our laughter.

We both turned and looked at this older woman who sat alone in the corner opposite us.

"I couldn't help but watch the two of you. You remind me of me and my husband. We used to come here once a year and do the same thing."

I looked to Bryce and smiled.

"That is wonderful. Is your husband getting your chocolate selection?" Bryce asked. "He really needs to get you the raspberry one." We both laughed and she gave a thoughtful smile.

"No, I'm afraid he isn't. I am here alone. He passed away five years ago. I make the trip here once a year, only on our anniversary. It fills my heart with the memories we shared, but I fear this may be my last year. My health hasn't been very good." She smiled at me, tears in her eyes.

"I'm sorry to hear that."

The lady nodded and looked down at her cup. "How long have the two of you been married?" she asked.

"Oh no, we're not married. We're just old friends," I blurted out, looking over at Bryce.

"Could have fooled me. You two have a certain...something. I can see it. The way you look at one another, the way your body language speaks to one another, you are going to get married." We both looked at one another. "I can tell. You see, you look at one another like me and my Charlie looked at each other. Give it time."

I looked at Bryce and him at me, a soft smile coming to his lips.

"I'm sorry if I made you both uncomfortable. I didn't mean anything by it." She began gathering her things. "I must be going. Enjoy your afternoon."

We both sat in silence, looking at one another as we watched her stand up from the table and make her way to the front door, waving and calling out good-byes to some of the girls behind the counter.

"That was weird. What do you say we make our way over to the antique shop you wanted to check out?" Bryce said, clearing his throat.

"Yes, let's."

We spent the afternoon, holding hands, wandering around town, and going in and out of all kinds of little shops. I made a couple of small purchases at the local bookstore. We were just about to call for the cab when we passed by the grocery store.

"We should probably grab something for dinner tonight," I said, grabbing Bryce by the hand and pulling him into the store.

Chapter Twelve

Bryce

When we arrived back at the house, Mia went to lie down after we put the groceries away, and I went to my office. I had been working away when I glanced at the clock on my desk. It was almost 6:00 p.m. I hadn't planned on working that long and hit send on one final email and shut my laptop down. While we had been out, Chase had called and needed a couple of documents I had stored on my computer so he could send them off to my clients. He had promised me he would take care of anything for me while he was at the office this weekend, so I could focus on relaxing.

I sat back in my office chair thinking about Mia,

wondering if she was still sleeping. We had spent a wonderful afternoon together, and for some reason, after only a couple of hours apart, I was already aching to be back beside her.

I didn't want to bother her just yet, though. I wanted her to rest, so I figured that I could at least make us a good dinner before the movie we had agreed on watching tonight.

I wandered into the kitchen and pulled out the two sirloin steaks we had purchased in town and busied myself seasoning them to perfection. Then I began working on the accompanying side dishes: sautéed mushrooms and onions and garlic mashed potatoes. While everything was cooking, I set the table, pulled my favorite Cabernet Sauvignon from the wine rack, and grabbed the candles from the drawer.

As I set them on the table, I could hear my ex's words in the back of my mind from that night that felt like forever ago.

"You're a selfish bastard. You make us dinner just to break it to me that you must go to work. You always expect me to keep everything up, and the one time in the last few months that you cook dinner for us, you can't even take the time to sit down and eat it with me."

Those words still haunted me, but it was so far from the truth that I didn't even know why they bothered me as much as they did. Regardless, I never wanted another person to think that way of me again, especially Mia. I don't know why I was worried about that or even thinking that way. Whatever this was, it was in no way the same thing. Mia and I had only just gotten reacquainted, and to be honest, after this weekend was over, who even knew if I would ever see her again.

Once the table was set and the side dishes were well on their way to being cooked, I turned the oven on and put the steaks in. I had planned to barbecue, but since we had been back, more snow had started to fall.

It wasn't long before the timer had gone off and dinner was ready. I shut the oven off and yelled down the hall to Mia to let her know dinner was ready while I plated the food. I placed the plates in our respective spots and sat waiting before realizing I had forgotten music and quickly set my phone to play a romantic mix of music.

I kept thinking I heard her coming toward the kitchen, but after waiting for ten minutes, I realized she wasn't coming and perhaps she was still asleep.

I got up from my chair and wandered down the hall. The bedroom door was still shut tight, and wild thoughts passed threw my mind of ways I could slowly wake her up. I pressed my ear to the door and could hear her muted voice, sounding frustrated.

Frowning, I reached for the doorknob and opened the bedroom door to find her buried under a mountain of paperwork, her hair a frazzled mess, and she looked exhausted and stressed. Her cell phone was pressed to her ear and she wore a very frustrated look on her face.

"No, you are not looking at it right. Column B, Mark, check column B," she mumbled under her breath.

She was just about to say something else when she noticed me standing there, watching her shove her hair away from her face in a panic. She placed her hand over the mouthpiece and whispered, "Bryce it's not a good time. I need to get this done. I can't talk right now." She huffed and went back into her phone call, shoving more papers around on her desk and barking instructions into the phone.

Instead of leaving, I leaned up against the doorframe and continued to watch her. She was so stressed there was no way I was leaving. There wasn't a job or career in the world that should get a person into a state like she was in right now.

She balled her fists and inhaled deeply, gritting her teeth at whoever or whatever was being said on the other end of the phone. Without another word, she hung up and threw her cell phone down on the desk. Gripping the back of the chair, she hung her head. There would be no more of this for her tonight. This vacation was not about this or whatever was going on back home at work for her.

I stepped into the room and placed both of my hands on her shoulders, gently massaging the tension she held there. I pressed my body against hers, inhaling the scent of her lotion, and closed my eyes while I continued to massage her shoulders. I wanted to bawl her out for not resting like she was supposed to have been. It looked like she had been working this entire time. Instead of saying what was on my mind I continued to massage her shoulders, until the tension in her body finally loosened.

"You know, I have this wonderful steak dinner ready in the kitchen for the two of us, a couple bottles of wine, and a rich chocolate cake from that bakery for dessert. I say you close everything down, shut off that cell phone, and come with me," I said, sucking her earlobe between my lips. "I promise to distract you from all of this."

I was more than prepared for an argument than I ever had been when she surprised me by doing exactly what I had suggested.

"You're right." That was all she murmured before she leaned back into me and took my hand in hers.

I reached and shut the light off and together we walked to the kitchen.

Two hours later, with full bellies, we were wrapped together in a blanket on the couch, with two empty wineglasses sitting on the table in front of us. We had shut the TV off long ago, and she lay beside me, wrapped in my arms, her leg over mine and her head on my chest while she traced tiny circles on my bare chest and watched the fire dance, the only sound in the room the crackle of the fire. I absolutely loved the feel of her fingers dancing over my skin.

"Feeling better?" I asked.

"Much. Thank you."

I kissed the top of her head and wrapped my arms around her tighter.

"Can I ask you a question?"

"Of course."

She went quiet, and I felt her swallow hard. She didn't lift her head to look at me. I just heard her tiny voice ask the question I had been praying she wouldn't ask.

"Earlier you said something about waiting for me. Why did you never..."

I closed my eyes. Those words had slipped out. She was never supposed to hear them. Me and my fucking alcohol.

"I mean, if you liked me, that is, then why did you never take a chance?"

I could feel the nerves creeping into my stomach as if I were still that sixteen-year-old boy standing in front of her, instead of the thirty-five-year-old man I now was. I let out a breath. "I wanted you from the first day I laid eyes on you. I remember it like it was yesterday. You came walking down the stairs in the hallway of your parents' house, you had on ripped jean shorts and a yellow tank top. You wore your hair up in this cute messy ponytail, pieces of hair falling in your face. Your brother introduced us, and I remember you walking into the kitchen and my eyes instantly flew to your ass, your shorts low enough that I could see the black thong you were wearing. I remember thinking how bad I wanted to sink my teeth into your ass in that moment. I went into your mom's bathroom five minutes later and snapped one off."

She let out a giggle. "No you did not."

"I did too. I couldn't contain it. My dick was harder than that coffee table. I think your brother new it, too, because before I left that night, he made it extremely clear to me that you were off-limits."

She grew quiet again. "So, basically, you didn't ever ask me out or anything because of him."

I scooted down on the couch, so we were eye level. I wanted to look into those beautiful brown eyes that had always so innocently stared up at me. As soon as our eyes met, I took her mouth, my hand resting on her cheek, and kissed her deep and slow. A wave of excitement ran through me as our tongues met. I gripped her ass and pulled her against me. She needed to feel me, feel what she was doing to me. As I pulled her close again, she let out a sexy groan that almost shook me to the core.

"Come with me."

"Where?" Mia asked, looking up at me as I stood up, bent down, and picked her up fireman style and headed toward the bedroom. "Bryce, put me down." She laughed all the way down the hall. I stepped into the bedroom and laid her on the bed.

"You stay there," I whispered, kissing her lips before I went and closed the bedroom door. I turned to see her sprawled across the mattress, looking sexy as hell. She was like a dream come true to me. My eyes swept over her body as I walked back to the bed and placed both of my hands on either side of her head and leaned down to meet her lips.

"Remember where we left off earlier?" I said quietly into her ear.

"Hmmm, yes."

I lay beside her, shutting off the bedside light so we were bathed in darkness. I pulled the covers over us and pulled her into me, kissing her. I felt her hand pull at the string on my house pants, loosening them enough so that she could slip her hand inside. She grabbed hold of my aching cock, and I felt her tiny hand start to jerk me, her thumb running through the bead of precum that sat so patiently waiting for her.

I closed my eyes and lay back against the pillow, and then I felt tiny kisses on my chest. I looked down and met her eyes as she continued trailing kisses down my abs. My hand ran through her hair as she continued her descent. She pulled on the waist of my pants, and I lifted just enough for her to pull them down, and then I felt her wet, warm mouth take my cock. She swirled her tongue around me and sucked with just enough pressure that I could already feel my keyed-up body threatening to explode.

"Baby, stop."

She pulled her mouth from me and looked up at me with lust-filled eyes. I reached over and ripped a condom from the drawer and laid back down on the bed. Within seconds, I had the condom on, and she sat there looking at me, a hint of mischief in her eyes.

I reached for her hands and pulled her over me. She straddled my lap as I lined my cock up with her entrance and she slid down onto it with ease. I could see the pleasure all over her face as I filled every inch of her. Her head fell back, and she bit her full bottom lip as she ground down on me.

"Bryce, I'm going to come."

It had only been a matter of seconds that her tight pussy had been wrapped around my cock, but I didn't wait. I reached down and started stroking her clit with my thumb, while I matched her rhythm.

"Stop, Bryce." She placed her hand on top of mine, trying to get me to stop rubbing her clit, but I kept going.

"No, Mia, come for me. Just let go," I bit out, fighting to hold back my own orgasm until she came.

She was so responsive, and for a little longer, I could tell she was trying to fight off her orgasm, but I could feel her tightening around me. I gripped her waist with my one hand while continuing to stroke her clit. She was soaked, and when she tightened around me this time, I was powerless to hold back and felt myself start to let go.

Her moans filled the room as the warm rush of heat escaped her. I pulsed inside of her, emptying myself, and she collapsed on top of me while those last few pulsing blows of my orgasm left my body. I held her in my arms, while we both caught our breath. I couldn't remember the last time that sex had felt like that for me.

My fingers stroked her back as she came down, and she finally eased off me and laid down on her side. I quickly got up and expelled the condom in the garbage and went and crawled back in beside her. Slipping my arm under her head, I pulled her body into mine and tugged the covers over us, and before I knew it, we both fell asleep.

Chapter Thirteen

Mia

I opened my eyes, the bright green numbers of the alarm clock staring at me. 10:45 a.m. I blinked hard and tried to remember what day it was. I sat up looking around the room, finding that Bryce was already up and gone. I grabbed my phone from the table. It was Monday. I had slept until almost 11:00 on a Monday morning, which was unheard of.

I slipped into my discarded clothing that was piled on the floor and left the room. The house was quiet, and I finally found Bryce in the kitchen. He had just poured himself a cup a coffee and grabbed another mug from the cupboard when I entered the kitchen.

"Good morning, sleepyhead," he said, bringing over the mug of hot coffee to me and kissing me on the cheek. "Sleep well?"

"Too well." I grinned.

"Great, that means you're starting to unwind. I'm going to help once again with that process. I'm taking you over to the spa. You have a mud wrap and massage in exactly one hour." He popped a piece of fruit into his mouth.

"That sounds amazing. What are you going to do while I am doing that?"

"No need to worry about me, but if you must know, I am going to enjoy the sauna while you are getting pampered. So, go get dressed," he said, handing me a bowl of fruit before leaving the kitchen." He slapped my ass as he walked by and winked at me.

I carried my mug, along with the fruit, with me down the hall, and just before I entered the room, I could already hear my cell phone ringing away. I set the mug and bowl on the table and grabbed my phone.

"It's 11:00! Where the hell are you? You were supposed to be here at 7:30."

"Who is this?"

"It's Mark, and it's Monday. Where are you?"

"I told you, I went on vacation."

"Mia stop joking around. This merger is everything,

and you are supposed to be here now. I need you here," Mark barked into the phone.

Bryce walked into the bedroom and glanced at me, a worried expression on his face. He didn't say anything; he just walked over to the closet and began searching for some clothes.

"Listen, I told you already, I haven't had a vacation in fifteen years. I have thousands of vacation hours banked, not to mention all those unpaid overtime hours. You can't deny me."

As the words fell from my mouth, I noticed Bryce had stopped what he was doing and now sat down on the edge of the bed. I could feel him watching my every move and listening to every word I was saying.

"I do the work of probably five, if not six, people. My department shouldn't just be me, Mark. Remember what I told you before I left. I meant it."

I hung up the phone and threw it into my purse, my head pounding. I sat down on the edge of the bed beside Bryce and rested my head on his shoulder.

"Who was that?" Bryce asked, placing his arm around me.

"My boss." I rubbed my eyes. "He's in a tizzy because of the merger that is happening."

"He needs you to work?"

"Well, of course, but I have been doing this straight for fifteen years with no break, the work of probably six people. He didn't believe me when I said I was going on vacation."

"Wait a minute, you're serious? You really haven't had a vacation in fifteen years? You do realize that is against the law, right? You must have close to twenty-three, twenty-four hundred hours banked. That is like a year's salary."

I laid back onto the bed and stared up at the ceiling. "Yep, and I have a pay stub to prove it too, along with about three years of overtime that hasn't been paid to me."

"What? He hasn't been paying you for your overtime either?"

I shook my head and sat back up, running my fingers through my hair. "He said to bank them and that I could have time off when needed, only they have just sat there accumulating because I never get time off." I blew out a breath. Just when I had begun to relax, as always, that luxury had been ripped away from me.

"Sounds to me like you need a lawyer. It just so happens that I know someone who would be more than happy to take on that case."

"No, I don't need a lawyer," I barked.

"Mia, what he is doing is against the law."

"It's okay, Bryce. He will calm down once everything settles down there. He says I will get paid out everything and not to worry." I reached into my bag, pulling out a pair of clean underwear and a bra. I grabbed the clothes I had already decided to wear for the day and bundled everything in my arms. "I'm going to hop into the shower."

"All right, you have an hour," Bryce said, watching me with a worried expression on his face.

I walked over to the bathroom, stepped inside, and shut and locked the door behind me. I just needed a few minutes to myself.

Twenty minutes later, I emerged from the bathroom, my hair wrapped up in a towel, and I sat down on the bed. I was starting to feel better already, and I dug through my bag to find my hairdryer. I was almost back to the bathroom door when my phone rang. I hesitated to answer at first but decided to anyway. As soon as I had the phone to my ear, I could hear Mark's angry voice pouring over the phone. "I need things, Mia, please."

"Mark! I told you—"

"No! I need those reports in two hours or else you are fired!"

Instantly the fight-or-flight response kicked in, and all the stress I had lost over the last three days was now back and stronger than ever. I went to say something back to Mark, but he was already gone. I dropped the phone onto the bed and forgot what I had been doing. I went over to the small desk where everything had been left yesterday and sat down and began working, quickly forgetting all about Bryce and my day at the spa.

Half hour later, I heard a gentle knock at my door,

followed by Bryce calling my name. I ignored him. My boss was pissed, and now I was on an even more serious deadline than before. I had struggled to hold onto this job, and I wasn't going to lose it now.

"Mia, we have to—" He stopped mid-sentence as he pushed the door open to find me still with a towel wrapped around my head. He stood in my doorway looking down at me. I didn't look at him. I couldn't. I hadn't even gotten dressed, still sitting in the bathrobe I had put on after my shower. Work, as always, won.

"Mia, we have to go," he repeated.

"I can't," I bit out, typing away on the keys of my laptop.

"Mia, I watched you last night nearly have a nervous breakdown over this job that has broken so many laws. Does your employer not care about your mental or physical health? Does he not know that this is actually a form of harassment?" he bit back, standing there with his hands on his hips. I could see the lawyer in him coming out.

"You don't understand, this is my job."

"No, I understand fully. I see an employer who is taking advantage of you and an employee who is so afraid of losing her job that she will do anything to prove to them she is worth keeping. Now you are going to put that laptop away after you write him and tell him you will get right on that paperwork when you return to the office at the end of your vacation and not a minute before."

"I can't!" I shouted, pushing the hair from my face.

"You can, it's simple."

"I will lose my job, Bryce."

"Mia, you are not going to lose your job."

"I will, he told me so. You aren't going to be the one to have to pick up the pieces, I am. So, I am sorry to disappoint you, but I can't continue on with this party."

I stood up and pushed him out the door, slamming it in his face. I sat down and put my head in my hands, sobs racking my body. I didn't need some guy I hadn't seen in years coming back into my life and telling me what was right or wrong. I let the crying continue for a couple of minutes before I sucked it up, wiped my eyes, and went back to my laptop.

I worked straight through the afternoon and most of the evening until everything was completed. I sent off the final email, my phone ringing as soon as I received the notification it had been delivered and read.

"Hello."

"Mia, I'm sorry, but I'm going to have to let you go," Mark's voice rang out over the phone.

"What? Why?" I asked, choking back tears.

"I wasn't kidding, Mia. You had a deadline. You missed it."

My heart sank. I had nothing to say, and even though I had just spent hours working away, pushing away the one person I so badly wanted to be with, it hadn't mattered. In the end, I still lost.

I didn't argue. I physically couldn't. I simply hung up the phone and got up from my chair and looked around at the mess before me, papers scattered everywhere. I was so defeated, I flopped onto the bed. All of this had been for nothing. I had been fired anyway.

In that second, my life, up to this point, flashed before my eyes. My mom was gone, I hadn't seen my brother in seven years, I had never met my niece or nephew, I didn't have a significant other in my life, and I had lost every single friend I had ever had, and all for what?

I thought back to the last few days here. They had been the best days I'd had in a long time, and I had just pushed it all away too. I wiped at the tears that had started to form in my eyes. I needed another shower.

I turned the water on and climbed in, letting the heat soak into my aching muscles. I was frozen, and so I turned the hot water on, reducing the cold. As I sat on the floor, letting the hot water run over me, I heard Bryce's words in my mind. I felt awful for how I'd treated him. He had been nothing but kind, and I had treated him like shit. All he had really done was show me that he cared enough to try to help me, which had been more than anyone else had done for me in a long while.

When I was as warm as I was going to get, I shut the

water off and dried off, quickly dressing and going in search of Bryce.

I poked my head out of the door and saw the light on in the front room, while the rest of the house was dark. At least I didn't have to look far, I thought as I made my way down to the doorway. The TV was off, soft music playing in the background, a single light on by the couch. Then I saw Bryce kick his foot up on the back of the couch. I wandered in and walked around to the face him. Bryce laid there reading a book.

"Hey." I sniffled.

"Leftovers are in the fridge, if you're hungry. Help yourself to whatever you want." He didn't look at me. He kept his face down in the pages of his book and said nothing more.

"Is everything okay?" I asked, sitting down on the edge of the couch beside him, resting my hand on his thigh, which he pulled away as soon as I touched him, as if I had burned him.

"No, not really, and I am not even going to try and pretend that it is."

A funny feeling crept into the pit of my stomach at the tone of his voice. I had been in this situation before. It was all too familiar to me. Don and I had these types of conversations numerous times before, each of them ending in a fight.

"Bryce, why won't you look at me?"

He kept his face down in his book, not necessarily ignoring me but not acknowledging me either. I started to get a sick feeling in the pit of my stomach.

"I'm sorry. I felt that was important to take care of, but it really doesn't matter now."

He slammed his book shut and threw it on the table. "Yes, I noticed. You should have seen yourself, or maybe you should have seen yourself the night before, too, when you were on the verge of having a nervous breakdown. You barked at me to go, so I left." Bryce sat up and rested his arms on his knees. "You know, Mia, you once had a backbone and would never let anyone walk on you the way they are walking on you. Open your eyes."

"I have a backbone, and I do stand up for myself. You need to understand, what I do at times needs to be fully explained because if the other person doesn't understand then I have failed. And it's my job! Who is going to pick up my life if I don't have one? Who is going to provide for me if I can't provide for myself? For me to blow him off so I can go and spend the day with the guy I've shacked up with for some weekend fling is completely irresponsible and it's not going to happen."

I could see the hurt in his eyes immediately after the words fell from my mouth. I instantly wanted to take them all back.

He didn't say anything. Instead, he got up from the couch, picked his book up from the table, and was just about to leave the room when he stopped and turned to look at me. "One thing I have learned over my years as a lawyer, there are ways of getting your point across without losing control. You had no control. I really hope the hours you spent behind that computer today makes a difference for you."

"Why do you even care, Bryce? Why do you even care how I am being treated?"

"I care because I hate seeing people get taken advantage of and I hate wasting my time, which I can plainly see I have done nothing with you but that. I was trying to show you there is more to life than paper and offices and deadlines. I'll be spending the night in my office. Don't bother coming down there. I think it's best that we both be alone tonight."

I watched him make his way back around the couch and go to leave the room. I wanted to scream, "Stop, don't go," but I couldn't. Tears filled my eyes, and just as he was about to step around the corner, a sob escaped my throat.

"I got fired," I blurted out. We were standing here hurting one another for nothing. None of it mattered anymore.

Bryce stopped and slowly turned around, looking at me. "What did you just say?"

"I got fired. You know what though? It's okay. Everything you have said to me this weekend has been true. None of it has been worth it. It wasn't worth it for me to throw away every friend I had. It wasn't worth it to not see my brother or meet my niece and nephew, and it wasn't worth it for me not to take the time to mourn the loss of Mom when she passed away either."

I flopped down on the couch, tears pouring down my cheeks. It was only a matter of seconds before I felt Bryce's arms around me, holding me. He pulled me into his chest, and I rested my head on his shoulder, and he held me until the tears finally stopped pouring.

It had been two hours and I was still sitting beside him, leaning into his chest, his arms still wrapped around me, running his fingers through my hair. The fire was now nothing but a bunch of glowing embers, the TV was on, casting a glow over the room, the light having been shut off a while ago. My chest was tight, and every once in a while, when I would inhale, I could still feel the upset within me.

"You need to talk to my brother. We will get this all sorted out," he whispered in my ear.

I didn't answer, but I thought about what he was saying.

"For real, Mia. He will make sure you get your job back."

I sat there thinking about what he was saying. "What if I told you I don't think I want it back." My voice was barely audible, even to me.

"Well, if you don't want it back, that is okay, but they still owe you a lot of money."

"What will I do though? It's all I have known."

"You will find another one, in time. There's no rush." He kissed my forehead, pulling me against him. "I think for now, though, we should get some sleep."

I nodded. Sleep sounded like a wonderful idea. The exhaustion from the last few hours was catching up to me.

He took my hand and pulled me up off the couch and we walked to the bedroom. I crawled into bed and pulled the covers over me. I just wanted to sleep everything away.

At first, I thought he had left the room, going to his office as he had said he would, but instead the light went off and I felt the opposite side of the bed sink. He pushed his arm under my head and wrapped his other arm around my waist, pulling me tightly against his chest and into the warmth and safety of his embrace.

Chapter Fourteen

Bryce

When I woke the next morning, I found her face buried in my side, tears streaming down her cheeks. I had done the best I could to comfort her, but this was a battle she needed to take care of on her own.

We ate breakfast, and then Mia asked me if it was okay if she had some alone time. I understood completely and gave her some directions to a trail out back of the house, and off she went for a walk.

I knew this had been hard on her. We had decided on something easy for dinner tonight, so I took some time while she was out to surprise her with my mother's beef stew recipe. She and Grant used to love it when we were younger. I had also pulled out all the ingredients for us to bake chocolate chip cookies later.

After I got the stew slowly simmering on the stove, I pulled out all the bowls and measuring cups from the cupboard for the cookies. I was expecting Mia to be back soon when something caught my eye out the back window. Mia was sitting down on top of the hot tub looking out toward the mountains. She looked lost in thought, and I was just about to go make my way out the back door when the phone rang.

I popped a handful of mixed nuts into my mouth and grabbed the phone, still watching Mia out the back window. "Hello."

"Bryce, how are things going?"

"Hey, Hunter. Doing much better, thanks," I said. I owed my brother a lot for sending me on this vacation. He had been right, as he normally always was.

"Good to hear. Are you doing okay with all the snow? We were getting a bit worried. We hadn't heard from you. Autumn forced me to check in with you."

I let out a laugh. "Good to know someone cares about me. Really there is no need to worry. Everything is just fine."

"Good to hear. You still planning on coming home this weekend? Autumn and Hope want to know if you will be here for family dinner."

"Yep, I'm coming home." I stood there debating telling him about Mia, my gut practically screaming at me to just go ahead and do it. "Listen, I ran into an old friend. Mia, Grant's sister. You remember her?"

Hunter chuckled into the phone. "Yeah, I remember. The looker who used to crush on you so bad it made my head spin."

I frowned. "She did not," I answered back.

"Yeah, whatever. The way she paraded around you? Carter and I always laughed whenever you and Grant hung out. She was like static cling, man. In a good way, that is. Don't hate us, but we took bets on when you were finally going to wake up your cock and notice her. We seriously thought perhaps it didn't work properly." Hunter let out a loud laugh.

I didn't say anything as I looked out the back window at Mia. She was gorgeous sitting there, the sun bathing her in a orange hue. Thinking back to those days—something I had done a lot of this week—never had I thought she crushed on me.

"Listen, I went by your condo the other day. I stopped in to check on things. It looks like Alyssa is gone," Hunter said, pulling me away from my memories.

"Good to know. We'll be heading back tomorrow. Nice to know I can return to my home."

"We'll?" Hunter questioned.

"Yes, Mia and myself."

"She is there with you? As in you shacked up with her for the week?"

I cleared my throat, getting tired of his behavior. "No we didn't shack up, Hunter. She was stranded at the airport. I simply offered her a place to stay."

"Sure...I am sure you did. You probably parked your car in the garage too." He chuckled.

I guess I deserved his response, after all the years I picked on him.

"I have a favor to ask of you. Mia needs some legal help from you, if you are so inclined," I said, being as vague as I could be. It wasn't my place to tell him what this was about; it was hers.

"No problem. She can talk to me at family dinner?"

I frowned. "At family dinner? I wasn't planning on bringing her."

"Well, you are now. Autumn just added an extra seat. We will see you then."

I let out a breath. "Okay, we'll be there."

We said our good-bye, and then I hung up the phone. I grabbed another handful of nuts, turned the burner down on the stove, and headed out the back door.

"Hey." Mia turned to look at me, a smile lighting up her sad eyes. "Dinner is cooking. I also have everything out to make those chocolate chip cookies you have been talking about," I said as I walked around to face her, forcing her legs open so I could stand between them.

"Sounds good." She wrapped her arms around my neck and rested her head on my shoulder.

"I just got off the phone with my brother. He said he is willing to help you." She was quiet. "He also said you used to have a crush on me." She pulled away and looked me in the eyes, her face going red. "Did you used to have a crush on me?" I brushed a strand of stray hair away from her eyes.

She nodded her head, her cheeks on fire with embarrassment. "Maybe a little." She held her forefinger and thumb close together and let out a cute little giggle. "Well, until you broke my heart, that is," she said, getting serious.

"I have no idea what you are talking about," I said, playing dumb and putting my hand to my chest in an innocent gesture. I seriously didn't believe that she crushed on me that long anyway, and I certainly wasn't expecting the next words that fell from her mouth.

"Mary Maguire's party, do you remember that?"

My breath caught. She really had crushed on me. What I had seen in her eyes that night had been the truth.

"Yeah, you remember." She let out a laugh. "It's okay, though. I dropped my friend like a hot cake." She winked at me.

"Listen, I feel like I owe it to you to tell you this, even though it happened years ago. That night, I was really searching for you. Your friend only got me up there because she said you were waiting for me. It was a ploy, a trick played on me. Apparently, your friend had a crush on me as well." She looked at me with curiosity.

"When I saw you in the door that night and the hurt in your eyes, I tried to run after you, but the crowd of people kept getting in my way. Then I saw you with Grant, and well, you know how that would have turned out. I tried to come after you after Grant left, before I went to school as well, but you were either ignoring me or weren't home."

"It's okay, Bryce. I got over you. It took three months, but after that, I forgot about you."

"Geez, thanks. Way to make a guy feel special!"

"Okay, well maybe I didn't forget all about you."

"Let's get inside and get those cookies baked, and after that have some food," I said, wrapping my arms around her waist and throwing her over my shoulder in true caveman fashion. I loved listening to her laugh as I smacked her on the ass and carried her into the house.

Throughout the afternoon, we talked about the past. We had laughed and laughed, Mia telling me all the things she used to do to try and get my attention. It had probably been one of the best days we had had here together, and I was so thankful to have her back in my life. Even if all we would ever have together was this week, it was enough for me. It would have to be.

"Grab the eggs and crack two into that bowl."

I watched Mia carefully pick up and crack the eggs, carefully removing the few pieces of shell that had fallen in. She poured the eggs into the cookie batter and then grabbed the flour.

"You know they do say that the one you are supposed to be with is usually right under your nose the entire time, right?" I said, stirring the batter together as she continued to pour the flour into the bowl little by little.

"Let's hope not. I don't want to marry my boss." She laughed, missing the bowl completely and spilling flour on the counter.

"That makes two of us because I don't want to marry my secretary. She is almost old enough to be my grandmother."

Mia scrunched up her face, and we both laughed while she dumped in another cup of flour.

"Seriously, though, who is *they*? You always hear it, they say this, they say that, but no one ever knows who *they* are." Mia took a drink of her wine and giggled.

"Yeah, and I think you have had enough wine there," I said, reaching for her glass and trying to take it from her, but she pulled it away and took another sip.

"Is that all the ingredients?"

"I believe so." I placed my hands in the bowl to mix everything together. "Oh no, wait, the chocolate chips."

Mia grabbed the bag and dumped some into the bowl,

laughing hysterically at my shocked expression. Soon the cookies were in the oven, the dishes in the dishwasher, and Mia was sitting up on the counter, swinging her legs, drinking her wine, looking adorably cute.

"Tell me, the first night we were here, how did you really end up in the bed with me?"

I let out a chuckle and shook my head. "A man never tells."

"Oh no, Malone, spill it."

"You begged me." I smiled sexily at her. "You begged me to stay."

"I did not."

"Oh, I am sorry to say you did. I will admit it was rather sexy the way you pouted your lips." I winked.

She wasted no time hopping off the counter and approaching me, a soft smile on her lips. How I wanted to kiss her... I don't know what was stopping me.

I could see something in her eyes. She wanted to say something, do something. I was just about to take the plunge, but we were interrupted by the oven timer. Instead we both jumped and reached for the oven mitts at the same time.

"You open the door. I'll get the cookies," she announced, tipping to one side as she giggled, a hiccup surprising her.

"No, sweets, better let me." I grabbed the oven mitt from her hand.

We plated the cookies and carried them into the living room along with our wine. Soon we were sitting in front of the fire, the TV on, laptop in front of us, and we munched away on the cookies we had made while we searched together for a return flight home.

Chapter Fifteen

Mia

We sat on the plane watching the in-flight movie and sharing a pair of earbuds. I had taken the window seat. I was snuggled into Bryce's side, and even though he had loaned me one of his hoodies before we left, I was still cold.

"I hope you're not coming down with something," he whispered to me as he felt my cheek. "You feel warm to me."

"I'll be all right. I'm sure it's nothing serious." I pulled the hood up around my neck and rested my head on his shoulder. I really didn't want this to end. I didn't want to be without him or his warmth for even a second, but we hadn't spoken about what would happen after we returned home. Even though I was returning home to no job, I really wasn't all that upset. Overall, it had been the best week I'd had in a long time, and I had learned that work wasn't everything.

Two hours later, we had landed back in Kings Cove and we made our way through the airport to the parking lot. We had both been quiet throughout the flight. I couldn't tell from the expression on his face if he was happy or sad that we were back.

We were approaching the first parking lot when Bryce stopped. "This is where I am parked," he gritted out. Maybe he did look a little sad.

"Oh, well, I guess this is it then," I said, looking down at the ground. A huge part of me didn't want him to go.

"You have my number, right?" I nodded. "All right, well, give me a call sometime, and make sure you get in touch with Hunter okay? He is expecting your call."

"I will." I swallowed hard. Why did this feel like the end to me?

Bryce didn't waste time. He dropped his one bag to the ground and pulled me against him for a hug. Then he grabbed his bag and started on his way to his car.

I watched him for a couple of minutes, he would turn around and come back, but he kept walking. When I could no longer see him, I turned the cart and pushed my luggage to where I had parked my car and made my way home.

The only thing on my mind was the same thing that had been on my mind since I had gotten home earlier today: Bryce. I had wanted to call him but was afraid that calling so soon would make me appear desperate. So instead of sitting and torturing myself, I did my laundry, made dinner, and by 10:30 p.m. I shut the TV off and made my way to my bedroom. I laid in the dark with the TV on, wrapped in my duvet, wishing it were his arms around me and not a stupid blanket. I was cold and had started to come down with a sore throat.

I stared at the green numbers on my alarm clock. It was almost 11:00. Mark had called and left a few messages apologizing and begging me to come back to work. I knew he was under a tremendous amount of pressure with the merger coming up, but he had fired me. I knew he was worried about his job and things didn't look good for the company nor for the company that was looking to acquire it. The meeting with the lawyers was set for the coming week, and I knew this made Mark extremely nervous. Before I called him back, I planned to have a conversation with Hunter as Bryce had suggested. I had already put a call in to him.

I thought long and hard while away about what direction I wanted to move in, especially after he had fired me. I was tired of being treated like garbage and tired of being taken advantage of by this company. Bryce had been right; it had just taken me this long to see it.

I let out a deep sigh, watching the little numbers turn on the clock, seconds feeling like minutes, minutes feeling like hours. It was going to be a long night. I wondered if Grant was working tonight. I hadn't spoken to him since before I had left for vacation.

I grabbed my cell phone and dialed my brother. I knew if he was busy it would go to voice mail, but I was happy that on the third ring a very sleepy voiced Grant answered.

"Hello."

"Grant, it's me. Did I wake you?"

"Mia?" His voice took on a questioning tone and he cleared his throat. "Is everything okay? I thought you were on vacation with what's his name. Give me a minute, will you?"

I heard the mumbled voice of June, his wife, in the background.

"No, it's not the hospital, baby, it's Mia. Go back to sleep," he said. "Yes, everything is fine with her. Go back to sleep."

I felt awful. I had probably woken up the whole house.

"Sorry, Mia. Is everything all right?" he asked, his voice taking on that worried tone again.

I couldn't blame him. I never called him this late at night, but I figured he would be at the hospital working.

"I'm so sorry, Grant. I didn't mean to wake you all up. I feel awful. How about I just call you in the morning?"

"No, Mia, it's fine. Everything is fine. I'm just coming off a very long fifteen-day stretch at the hospital. Are you back from vacation already?"

I figured I would be okay, but the second he had uttered those words, my throat got tight and I broke into tears. Everything that had happened over the past week had made me second guess everything in my life up to this point.

"It was awful. Don broke up with me, the snowstorm messed up all my plans." I went silent, wondering if I should tell him about Bryce. I sniffled, the build-up of pressure in my sinuses causing a bad headache.

"Oh, Mia, I am so sorry. Are you okay?"

That did it, I couldn't hold back anymore. The tears started to freely pour down my face. "I can't continue this pace in my everyday life. It's killing me. You were right, Grant, I'm a mess." I continued sobbing into the phone.

"Mia, I don't want to sound like an inconsiderate brother, but...do you want or need a referral to see someone? I have friends..."

He had friends all right. His so-called friend had put

me into this state. I kept quiet because I knew that wasn't what he meant. He had begged me to seek help after Mom had passed and when I had told him I was having a tough time at work. He didn't persist. He just told me to let him know if I needed help.

"I'll be fine, Grant."

"It's not a problem, Mia. If you do need someone, let me know. It will only take me a second to process a referral."

"I know. I was calling because I wanted to let you know I got fired while I was away. I am seeking the help of a lawyer."

"Good. I told you, what this company is doing is illegal. Who are you going to talk to?"

"Hunter Malone."

"Ahh, the good old Malone boys! Great choice. What made you decide to go with him?"

I cleared my throat and looked up at the ceiling. "Bryce." I held my breath. I wasn't sure what my brother was going to say to that.

"I didn't know that you still spoke to Bryce. How is he?"

"He's good. I haven't kept in touch with him. I ran into him at the airport the night Don broke up with me. I spent the week at his lake house when the storm stranded us." I got quiet again, deciding if I should continue about everything that had happened. Grant must have sensed that.

"Is there anything else you wanted to talk about?"

I chewed my bottom lip, staring up at the ceiling. There were so many things I wanted to talk about: the kids, visiting him, and Bryce.

Grant didn't say anything. Instead he waited for me to continue.

I was quiet, the words almost burning my tongue at what I wanted to ask him. "If I told you that I had the best time of my life this week with Bryce, would you be okay with that?"

I heard him take a drink of something and swallow hard. "I would. Why wouldn't I be? I mean, I seriously can't think of anyone better to help you out and look after you than Bryce. We've kept in touch over the years. He is a good man. And you are right to get in touch with his brother. He's a damn good lawyer. I don't think any of them would ever steer you wrong."

"No, Grant, you are missing what I am asking?"

"What are you asking, Mia?"

"Well, it's just I had such a good time with him. I guess what I am asking is if you would be upset if I wanted to start seeing him?"

Grant was quiet. I could hear him breathing, so I knew he was still there. I didn't say anything else. I just waited for him to answer me.

"How much of a good time did you have while you were away?" he asked, chewing on something.

I let out a little giggle at his question. "I'm not sixteen, Grant, and what I did or didn't do with him is none of your concern. But your approval is important to me, that's all."

"I never said anything!" he exclaimed. "And I know you're not sixteen. Do whatever makes you happy, Mia. That's all I want to see."

I grew quiet. I missed my brother so much. "Grant?"

"Yeah?"

"If I wanted to come out and visit sometime in the next couple of months, would that be okay?"

"Mia, of course. We told you anytime. We would love nothing more than to have you here."

"Really?"

"Yes. Jeanna's birthday is coming up. She's going to be five. I know that both the kids would love to finally meet their aunt. If you can make it happen, how about you come out for that?"

I swallowed hard, fighting back the tears. "Okay, I think I can do that," I whispered, my throat getting tight.

"Sounds like a plan then. And honestly, if you had that great of a time with Bryce and something develops, I will be happy for you."

Grant and I talked for a little while longer. He shared with me what had been going on at the hospital and with the kids, and I shared a few highlights of my vacation with Bryce. Actually, I hadn't been able to keep his name from my tongue. I figured Grant would more that likely notice, and if he had, he never said anything. We finally got off the phone an hour later, and I could barely keep my eyes open and fell into a deep sleep.

Chapter Sixteen

Bryce

I glanced down at my watch to see it was only 10:00 in the morning. I had been busy working away on the upcoming merger since I had gotten into the office this morning, but my stomach was already growling. I dialed Hunter's extension to see if he could get out for some lunch. Chase had already turned me down, saying he had a lunch date with his newest conquest.

"Hunter."

I could tell he was concentrating on something when he picked up; the tone of his voice told it all.

"Hey, you able to get out for lunch today. Thought

maybe Willow's Landing might be a good place. I'm dying for the chicken salad."

"Wish I could. Autumn has a doctor's appointment this afternoon, and I promised her I would go with her. Plus, I have an appointment with Mia in the next forty minutes, and I already know she is going to have a ton of questions."

I perked up at Mia's name. I hadn't seen her since we parted ways at the airport. We had been in touch through text, but that was all.

"All right, man, I have to go. My next appointment is here anyways. Good luck with your doctor's appointment."

"Oh, before you go, Autumn just wants to confirm that you will both be there tomorrow night."

I rolled my eyes. I still hadn't asked Mia. I needed to get off my ass and talk to this girl and stop being a coward.

"Yes, of course, we will both be there," I answered him, clearing my throat. Once we hung up, I picked up my cell phone and quickly sent a text to Mia asking her to call me. My phone rang almost instantly, Mia's name flashing across my screen. "Hello," I answered.

"Hi, I am just on my way to see your brother. What's up?" her cheery voice came over the phone. I was glad to see she was in better spirits.

"Listen, how would you like to have lunch with me today?" I swallowed hard. Last week, I had been balls deep in this woman, and now suddenly I was nervous about asking her to lunch. This didn't make sense to me.

"Of course, I would love to. Where should we go?"

"How about I just meet you in the lobby after your meeting?"

"Sure thing. I guess I'll see you soon then." I could tell she was smiling. I could hear it in her words, and I couldn't wait to see her face.

I worked through the next fifty minutes with an extra spring in my step and couldn't help but keep glancing at the clock all through my appointment. I knew that I would be seeing my girl soon. Just knowing she was in the building was enough to have my heart beating wildly in my chest.

"Jon, I guess I will get all these documents drawn up and sent to you via email in the next couple of weeks. Sound good?" I said, walking my client to the door.

"Sounds great, Bryce." He reached out and shook my hand.

"If you have any questions, feel free to call or email me."

I turned and walked back to my desk, my phone vibrating across the wooden top. "Hello, Bryce," I said into the mouthpiece.

"I'm waiting. You said in the lobby, right?" I heard her soft, sexy voice ask, the sound of it going straight to my cock.

"I'm on my way."

I ran out of my office and to the elevator, Janice looking at me. "Bryce, slow down."

"Sorry, Janice, just on my way to meet a friend for lunch. I'll probably be a little late coming back, so please reschedule my one o'clock." At least, I hoped I would be late, I thought to myself as I stepped into the elevator and made my way down to my girl.

We took a seat at Willow's Landing, Mia sliding into the booth across from me. She wore this little black dress with knee-high boots and a bright-blue scarf around her neck that set off her eyes. The dress wrapped around her body, accentuating all the best parts of her.

"What did you want to eat?" I asked, studying her as she read the menu.

Those pretty eyes looked up from the menu, and she bit her bottom lip—the same lip that not a week ago I had sucked on.

"Did you feel like sharing something? I haven't been very hungry lately."

"What did you have in mind?" I took a drink of my water and placed the glass back down on the table.

"I have a severe craving for nachos."

"You got it. Did you also want to split a chicken salad?" I asked, closing my menu and dropping it onto the table.

She nodded her head and smiled at me, setting her

menu off to the side as well. Soon we had our salad and nachos and both of us dug in.

"So I have a question for you, and I hope it doesn't seem too forward. If it does, just tell me no, and we will move on." I was rambling and I knew it.

"Go for it. After all, how much more forward can we get? You have seen me naked." She laughed and popped a chip into her mouth.

"Would you like to be my date tomorrow night?" I asked, hoping to avoid telling her where we were going.

"Um, sure. What is it, a work function? What do I need to wear?" she asked, pulling out her phone. "Oh and time?"

"Ah, I will pick you up at say 5:00. Dress casual. Jeans and T-shirt are fine."

She looked at me and smiled, tilting her head. "Bryce, where are we going?"

"How did your meeting with Hunter go?"

"Oh no, no way. You aren't getting off that easy. Are you asking me out on a date? Where are we going?" she said, resting her hand on top of mine, and I was trying hard to ignore her question. "Bryce?"

"Okay, okay, it's just my family dinner. I made the mistake of telling Hunter when we were back at the lake house that I had run into you, and Autumn asked me if I would bring you. I told her yes without even thinking twice." I shrugged.

"I see." She wiped her hands on her napkin and looked down at them.

"If you don't want to go, it's okay. I will just make up something." I shrugged, taking a sip of my coke.

"It's not that, Bryce. I want to go. I'm just surprised it took you this long to ask me. That's all." She shrugged, picking up another chip.

"It's not because I didn't want to. I guess I was afraid of the answer I might get."

"Why? Did you think I would say no?"

I shrugged. I wasn't exactly sure what I thought she would say. "I guess I thought you might say no." I swallowed.

She looked at me, the light dancing in her eyes, and shook her head. "I don't think I could ever utter those words to you," she whispered.

Chapter Seventeen

Mia

I fiddled with my hair in the bathroom mirror. I never understood why it was that when you had somewhere important to go there was always one strand of hair that just wouldn't co-operate.

I took my round brush, trying to get it to curl the way I wanted it to, and finally giving up, I tucked it behind my ear. I checked my makeup, making sure that it looked perfect. I walked out of the bathroom and picked my favorite pair of jeans up off the bed, slid them on, and checked my ass out in the full-length mirror. Then I threw on a black top and gave myself a onceover, finally completing the outfit with my knee-high black boots. I gave myself another onceover in the mirror, letting out a breath to calm my nerves.

I was heading down the hall to the living room when I heard a knock on the door. I glanced at my watch: quarter to five. I grabbed my purse and keys from the table and my jacket and headed to the door, pulling it open to see Bryce standing on the porch.

He was dressed in blue jeans with a black sweater that hugged him in all the right places, his three-quarter length jacket hanging open. His eyes ran over me, taking in all my curves.

"Hey, gorgeous, you ready to go?" he asked, holding his hand out for me to take.

"Yep. Let me grab my jacket. Give me the rundown again of who will all be there."

He helped me with my coat, and we left the house, locking the door on the way out.

"All right, so, Carter and Hope and their kids, Kendall, Mackenzie, and Carl. Then there is Hunter and Autumn and their daughters, Kaylee and Paige. Then Chase. I don't know who he is dating today. Most of the time he shows up alone. Mom may be there. Hunter wasn't sure if she was coming or not. She normally plays bridge with her ladies club tonight."

I let out a breath and fiddled with the strap on my purse as Bryce drove us over to Carter's place. I kept seeing Bryce watching me out of the corner of my eye. Finally, he reached over and placed his hand on top of mine to stop me.

"Are you nervous?" He chuckled.

"Maybe." I shrugged. "It's been a long time since I have seen everyone."

"It will be good for you. And you have already seen Hunter, so it's like you have been reacquainted with two of us."

The car ride wasn't nearly as long as I had hoped for when Bryce pulled into the driveway of a two-story home. The gardens were perfectly landscaped, not a thing out of place. He shut the engine off.

"You ready?"

I searched around frantically in the front seat, looking over my shoulder into the back seat.

"Mia, what are you looking for?"

"We can't go in. The cookies I baked for dessert aren't here. I must have left them on the counter at home."

"It's fine. Hope would kill you if you brought anything, and so would Autumn. I brought wine. You can give it to them. Sound good?" he said, rubbing the back of my hand, trying to calm me down.

I nodded. I had just shut the car door when the front door opened and four girls came bounding down the front steps screaming, "Uncle Bryce!" They all shouted, running around and crashing into him. He took a second and gave each one of them a huge hug. They were all talking, telling him something different or wanting him to look at this or that, and he acknowledged them all, never missing a beat.

I didn't know how he kept up. Then, just like that, they were gone, running back to the house screaming for their parents.

"Sorry about that. They get a little crazy." Bryce laughed, coming around to my side of the car. He held out the bottles of wine he had picked up and gave them to me. "Ready."

I let out the breath I was holding once again, and we walked up to the front of the house. I could already hear everyone inside, talking and laughing. The kids were screaming. It was overwhelming, considering I didn't come from a large family to start with.

"We're here," Bryce announced, stepping inside and removing his shoes, and I followed, slipping my boots off and tucking them neatly into the corner.

"'Bout fucking time, you shithead," Chase said, getting up from his seat and smacking Bryce on the back.

"Chase, your language," a very pretty and very pregnant brunette scolded.

"Sorry, Autumn. I forgot about little ears." He chuckled and went back to take his seat.

"I'm Autumn," she said, coming right over to me. "Hope is in the kitchen. You must be Mia." She wrapped her arms around me and hugged me. "It's so nice to meet you."

"We brought some wine," I said, handing her the two bottles.

"Oh, what I wouldn't give for a drink right now," she whispered more to me than anyone else. "After the baby comes, look out." She laughed.

"I heard that." Hunter laughed, coming in behind Autumn and resting his hands on her sides. "Good to see you again, Mia," he said, placing a kiss on his wife's neck. "Soon enough, baby, soon enough, you'll get to have a drink. At least, I hope anyways. I have been cut off until this little one arrives." Hunter winked at me and continued into the dining room.

Autumn rolled her eyes at me. "He sneaks into the office every night and has a glass of scotch. He thinks I don't know, but I do."

I couldn't help but let out a laugh. Autumn took the bottles and disappeared into the kitchen. Bryce placed his hands on my hips and guided me into the dining room. He went around to what must have been his usual seat and pulled the chair that was beside his out and waited for me to take a seat.

"How is that brother of yours?" Chase asked once we were both seated.

"He's good. He's married to a woman named June.

They met in medical school, and they have two kids: a boy, Thomas, and a girl, Jennifer," I answered.

"Do you see them much? He moved out west, didn't he?"

"Yes, Sacramento. He works at the Shriners Hospital for Children." To be honest, I hadn't a clue what my brother really did at the hospital. All I knew was that his hours were long, and he was normally always busy.

"Ah, you must be Mia."

I turned my head to see a beautiful blonde woman coming toward me carrying a dish of something that smelled yummy. She placed the dish on the table, and then came around and hugged me.

"I'm Hope, Carter's wife. Welcome to our home. We are thrilled to have you join us tonight."

I hugged her back, swallowing hard. "Thank you so much for inviting me."

"Well, when Autumn heard the excitement in Bryce's voice when he spoke of you, we knew we had to."

I glanced over to Bryce, the hint of pink in his cheeks telling me that was the truth. He had been talking about me. A warm feeling settled in the pit of my stomach.

"All right, sis. That's enough. Let's get on with dinner," Bryce said, clearing his throat.

I sat back down. This was almost too much for me. I looked to Bryce for help, and when his eyes met mine, he winked and mouthed, "You're doing great," and placed his hand on my thigh, giving it a squeeze of reassurance. Then he joined in the conversations with his brothers as if that hadn't even happened.

I was quiet throughout dinner. Everyone was talking amongst themselves. Hunter and Carter tended to the girls and helped them all with their dinner so that Hope and Autumn could eat in peace. It was so nice to see families working together; it was something I had never had. This brought me back to when Grant and I were kids and would join the Malones for family dinner. We were always made to feel welcome and as if we were part of their family.

Hope and Autumn busied themselves cleaning up the table after everyone had eaten. I went to help by grabbing two of the dinner plates, but Hope stopped me.

"No way, Mia. First meal here. You are our guest, and I won't have you help with anything, so you sit down. Next time will be different," she said, smiling and reaching for the plates I had piled together.

Chase had excused himself to take a phone call, and Hunter and Carter were busy with the other kids for a second. I leaned into Bryce's shoulder.

"You okay?" he whispered.

I looked at him and saw the happiness dancing in his eyes. I nodded. He placed his arm around the back of my chair and kissed me on the cheek when he was sure no one was looking.

Soon we were all seated back at the table, a slice of chocolate cake sitting in front of each of us and a steaming hot cup of coffee to go with it. The kids were off playing in the living room. Next thing I knew, Kendall and Kaylee were standing beside Bryce, holding a picture from one of their coloring books in their little hands.

"What do you want, girls?" Autumn asked, taking a sip of her herbal tea.

They held the picture above Bryce's head—a picture of cupid. "It's almost Valentine's Day. Cupid came to visit. You have to kiss the girl next to you," they sang as Bryce looked above his head.

He wrapped his arms around the girls and kissed them on their cheeks. "Noooooo..." they squealed. "You have to kiss her," they sang, pointing to me.

I could feel my cheeks getting warm as Bryce looked to me. "What will happen if I don't?" he asked.

"No more kissing ever," Kaylee sang out.

"It's true," Autumn said, winking at the girls.

Bryce looked over at me. "You heard them. Can't have that happen." He winked and leaned in and kissed me on the cheek. I could feel everyone looking at us, the heat in my cheeks making me feel as if I were on fire.

"Nooooooo!" the girls shouted. "Like Mommy and Daddy!" Kaylee shouted.

Hunter let out a laugh. "Yeah, Bryce, that was pretty

weak. Don't force me to show you up." He laughed, winking at me.

Bryce turned back to me and placed his hand on my cheek, pulling me into him. His lips met mine, and I felt his tongue sweep through my mouth. The kiss was interrupted by a bunch of cheering little girls. Bryce slowly pulled away from me. I could tell he wanted more just from the look in his eyes. I wanted more, too, the throbbing at my center letting me know that loud and clear. The girls quickly moved on to Chase holding the picture above his head.

"All right, girls, that's enough now. Go and play," Hope said to the pair of them.

Their little faces turned into pouts as they wandered into what must have been the living room.

"Thank God, you saved me," Chase said, wiping his brow. "I have no one to kiss. I can't lose that for the rest of my life."

We all laughed.

"You have more practice than the three of us combined." Hunter chuckled.

"You're lucky they left because it would have been your wife I kissed," Chase said, winking at Autumn and laughing. "She'd have left your sorry ass in a heartbeat once I got hold of her."

The table erupted into laughter.

The evening continued, and before I knew it, Bryce

had looked down at his watch. I glanced over to see it was almost 10 p.m. The girls had finally settled down—Hunter had put a movie on for them in the other room—and we were just sitting around talking. It was as if I had always been a part of this family.

"What do you say we get going?" Bryce said, leaning in to me.

I nodded. I didn't want the night to end, but at the same time, I knew everyone was tired. Chase had left two hours earlier after he had gotten a call from what Bryce was sure was his next lay and had so expressed that to the dinner table.

"Guys, I think we are going to head out," Bryce announced, standing up and pulling my chair out for me.

Hunter and Carter looked to their brother, knowing smiles on their faces. "We know what that means," Hunter said. "Going to get yourself a little action."

Autumn reached over and smacked him on the shoulder. "Enough," she gritted out, smiling at him.

"What? What did I say?" he asked, playing innocent.

"Let's go before my brother has us doing the nasty on the dining room table here," Bryce said, placing his hand on the small of my back and guiding me to the door.

We said our good-byes, and I thanked Hope and Carter for having me at dinner tonight. We walked to the car, Bryce coming around my side to open the door for me. His hand on the handle, I turned into him and met his lips. He slowly let go of the car door, pinning me up against the car and wrapping his arms around me to grip my ass and pull me closer. We must have stood there for five minutes, Bryce kissing down my neck, before he finally whispered in my ear, "Your place or mine?"

Chapter Eighteen

Mia

We decided to go to Bryce's place. After all, it was closer. We stepped into the elevator, and as soon as the doors had closed, he pushed me up against the wall, undoing two of the buttons on my shirt, kissing the tops of my breasts as they spilled out of my bra. I let out a moan as his lips danced over them and up to my neck.

The ding of the elevator stopped us. He pulled me out of the elevator, and we quickly walked down the hall to his condo door. Pushing me up against the wall while fishing in his pocket for his keys, he continued to kiss me, sucking my bottom lip into his mouth.

Finally, he pulled his keys out and fiddled around, trying to get the key in the lock.

"You never had this problem before," I moaned.

"What problem?" he asked, kissing my neck.

"Getting it in," I whispered into his ear.

"Believe me, in a few minutes I won't."

I heard the key slide into the lock, and he opened the door, pulling me inside and locking it behind us. I could feel the tension building in me at the thought of feeling him inside of me again, this time without the influence of alcohol. We kicked our shoes off and dropped our jackets in a pile at our feet.

He pushed me up against the wall and took my mouth, running his tongue across mine, his hands coasting over my body. I felt him grip the bottom of my shirt and his fingers danced over my skin, sending shivers through my body as he lifted my shirt over my head and let it drop at our feet.

He ran his thumbs over my bra, my nipples getting instantly hard at his touch that sent a hard pulse right to my center. I closed my eyes, allowing my other senses to feel his touch. I watched as he pulled his sweater up over his head, exposing his chest to me, and I ran my hands over his abs. Once he dropped his shirt to the floor, he grabbed me and pulled me against him.

He hoisted me up and wrapped my legs around his waist as he carried me down a hallway while he continued to consume my mouth. Next thing I knew, he had dropped me down onto his bed and stood over me, looking down on me. His lust-filled eyes swept over my body, his hand reaching down and flicking the front clasp of my bra open. He bent down and licked my left nipple, taking it between his teeth and gently biting it. I arched my back up off the bed, begging for him to do it again as he stood back up and once again looked down on me.

He reached down and gripped his cock through his jeans, and then quickly flicked the button open on his pants and let them drop to the floor, the buckle of his belt making a loud noise.

He stood over me, one hand on his thick, raging cock. I couldn't help but keep my eyes focused on his raging erection, thinking about what it would be like to take him in my hands, in my mouth, in my—

Before I could do anything, both of his hands were on my hips, his fingers tracing along the waist of my jeans, teasing me. He undid the button of my jeans and reached underneath me, and with one swift rough pull, he ripped them off me, along with my panties. He looked down at me longingly and placed one hand on each side of my head, bracing himself as he leaned over and teased my lips, first with his lips and then with his tongue.

Every part of this kiss was different—the way it felt, the way it made me feel, and the way it made my body hum. I couldn't recall ever being kissed like that before, and I felt a surge of wetness and hot, heavy throbbing at my center.

He grabbed my legs, bending them, so I was open to him. He held himself with one arm still bent over me, while his other hand found my center, and his fingers danced over my clit, stroking me with just the right amount of pressure.

"I'm a very selfless lover, Mia, and I will always make sure you are fully satisfied before you ever even think of touching me or pleasuring me," he said, almost moaning.

His eyes were hooded now, desire running through them. He dropped to his knees and pulled me closer to the edge of the bed and buried his face between my legs. I sat up on my elbows to watch him, but as soon as his tongue connected with me, my head dropped back, and I gripped handfuls of the blanket that was beneath me. I tried hard to stifle the moans he was causing, but I failed, and I began to scream his name out with every flick of his tongue against my clit.

With every stroke of his cock he took me higher and higher. As I moaned out my pleasure, he continued running his thumb rhythmically over my swollen and sensitive clit, gently coaxing my third orgasm of the night from my tired body. He kept going, burying himself deeper and deeper inside of me, my screams getting louder and louder, until he collapsed on top of me, emptying himself into the condom. Breathing hard, he rolled off me and collapsed onto the sheets beside me.

I felt the bed move and felt the absence of Bryce. I didn't have the strength to move. I could barely open my eyes and look around the room. We had spent the night in and out of sleep, and every once in a while, I would feel him wrap his arm around my waist and grind his hard cock into me, which would begin another bout of sex, this last one lasting almost forty minutes. The sun was just beginning to come up, casting a soft glow throughout the bedroom. I could see the blankets and sheets were somewhere on the floor and I giggled to myself. I hadn't been with a man like him before. Most of them were passed out after the first five minutes, never to wake until the sun was long up, leaving me to take care of myself.

"What's so funny?" Bryce asked, returning to the bed and picking up the extra pillows and blankets from the floor.

"It looks like we threw a party in here," I murmured, looking around at the mess of blankets on the floor.

"Don't worry about it," Bryce said, adjusting his pillows and placing his arm behind his head, his other hand resting on his delicious eight-pack as he lay back. I snuggled into his side, trying to fight off sleep.

"You certainly weren't kidding," I whispered.

"About?"

"About you not being a selfish lover."

He chuckled, and I felt the bed move and the heat of his body getting closer as he rolled onto his side. He lay there looking into my eyes, then pressed his lips to mine. I felt his fingers begin to trace little circles on the top of my leg, getting closer and closer to my center. They finally made their way, and I felt two of his fingers run through my wetness.

"Bryce, stop."

"Come on, one more time for good measure before I have to leave for the office." He leaned down and took my nipple into his mouth, causing me to let out a moan and my legs to relax enough that he could run his fingers through my wetness.

He kissed his way down my soft belly and crawled between my legs again, his hands forcing them apart. I studied the way he took me in. With his hands forcing me open, his mouth met my center, his tongue working my very sensitive clit, slowly and gently sucking and licking. I could already feel my orgasm starting to build. He slid two fingers gently inside of me, and I let out a loud moan as his tongue continued to lick repeatedly over my swollen clit.

My cell phone started ringing, and I placed my hands

on his head, signaling for him to stop as I went to reach for it.

"No, Mia, don't you even think about answering that," he growled and buried his face back between my legs.

The ringing stopped for only a second and started again. I looked over to the nightstand and reached for the phone.

"If you answer that, I won't stop. I will make you come into that phone receiver screaming my name. I doubt whoever is on the other end of the line will want to hear that, unless it's your ex. Which maybe in that case you should answer it. He should know what you really sound like when you truly come."

I started to laugh, my head falling back onto the pillow as he continued torturing me, my legs trembling. I dropped my phone on the floor, quickly forgetting about it as I felt my orgasm building. As he coaxed the last bit of my orgasm out of me, he rolled onto his back and I collapsed against the mattress.

"Fuck, Mia, you are so fucking hot when you come. I can't get enough of you."

I looked over at him as he ran his fingers through his messy hair. I could see his hard cock once again straining under the sheets. I sat up and ripped the sheet off him, my eyes landing on his cock. I ran my tongue over his hard abs, alternating between little licks and kisses.

"Mia, what are you doing?"

I said nothing and continued making my way down, finally taking his cock in my hand, running my hand over his shaft. I couldn't help it, I loved watching his face, the way he sucked his bottom lip between his teeth, the sound of his breath as he inhaled when I ran my tongue over the head of his cock.

"Put your mouth on me." He moaned as I continued stroking him.

I did as he asked and took his whole cock in my mouth, running my lips and tongue over him. I could taste the saltiness of his precum as I took his cock in my mouth. I felt his hand run through my hair and I opened my eyes, looking up at him. He was watching me, studying my face while I had his cock in my mouth. I felt him start to pulse and kept my eyes locked with his, and before I knew it, I felt him pour his cum into my mouth.

Bryce walked into the kitchen dressed in suit pants and a white button-down shirt, his tie hanging loosely around his neck, and his suit jacket flung over his arm. I greeted him with a smile as he lay the jacket down on the back of the chair.

"All ready?" I asked.

"I wish I didn't have to go in this morning. We could have spent the morning in bed." He came up behind me and buried his face into my neck. I let out a little giggle as his breath tickled my neck.

"I don't think I could handle much more," I answered shyly.

"Want to bet? What do you have planned for today?" he asked, taking the coffee from me while I went back to cooking us some eggs.

"Head home, shower. Look for a job."

"You can always shower here if you like."

"It's okay. I need to get some clean clothes anyways."

I placed the plates down in front of us and sat down beside Bryce. He took my hand in his and rubbed the back of it with his thumb.

"Listen, how about after I'm done working, I come home, get changed, and we go out for a romantic dinner, just the two of us."

"Sounds great. What did you have in mind?"

"It's a surprise."

"A surprise? How will I know what to wear?"

"All right, I will give you a hint: dress to kill." He winked at me, took a sip of coffee, and dug into his breakfast.

Chapter Nineteen

Bryce

I strode up the walkway to Mia's house. It was a cute little bungalow with great curb appeal and beautiful gardens. I held a dozen red roses in my hand and rang the bell. Seconds later, Mia appeared. She looked stunning, the black cocktail dress she wore hugging every curve, and the black heals she wore accentuating her legs perfectly. As my eyes danced over her, I couldn't help but hope for a repeat of last night. I held out the roses for her and she smiled as she took them from me and buried her nose into them.

"These are beautiful."

"They're okay. You're the beautiful one."

She smiled, holding the door open for me. "Let me put these into some water before we go."

I couldn't help but watch as she walked away from me, those curvy hips swaying.

"So where are we going?" she asked from the kitchen.

"The Cellar. We have reservations at 7:00."

"Sounds great," she said, walking back into the living room.

"Did you happen to pack an overnight bag?" I asked casually.

She blushed at my question and slightly nodded her head. "Is that okay?" she asked, crinkling her nose.

I pulled her into me, kissing her on the cheek. "Baby, it's more than okay." I grinned. "We should get going."

We were seated exactly at the table I had requested, the view overlooking the falls of Kings Cove the best in the entire restaurant. We had placed our orders and were waiting on our appetizer. Mia sipped her wine as she looked out over the water, a soft smile coming to her lips.

"It's beautiful here," she whispered to me.

"That it is." I studied her expression. She was gorgeous, and I was so lucky to have run into her again. I felt alive again. That part of me that had died when Alyssa and I split was now back.

A part of me was a little afraid to share how I really felt, but at the same time, I needed to. I had only spent a week and an amazing evening and night with this woman, but I couldn't deny how I felt. I wanted her with me, I wanted to come home to her, share things with her.

We made our way through dinner, talking and laughing. I shared my frustrations over the case I was working on, something I had never done with Alyssa. Somehow, I felt I could trust Mia, and she wouldn't judge me. She listened attentively, never offering her opinion, something my previous relationship lacked. She shared with me her challenges of trying to find a new job. She also shared with me what she and Hunter had spoken about. They had a damn good plan, and I couldn't wait to hear how it all went over.

"So, when is your big meeting?" I asked, as she brought the forkful of cheesecake to her lips.

"Tomorrow."

"Are you doubting yourself?"

"No, I just hope that we do the best we can for this client. That is all I ever want." I sipped on my espresso. "What about you?"

"Tomorrow as well. I'm meeting Hunter in the morning at the coffee shop around the corner from work."

"Okay, so I say that after the day we have a long, stress-free night. We can kick back, watch movies, and make some meatballs." I chuckled. "I'm actually dying to have those again, by the way."

"It's a plan." Mia ate the last forkful of her cheesecake and smiled at me. "Your place or mine?"

"Either, doesn't matter to me."

"All right, tomorrow night, it's my place then."

I put the key in the lock and held the door for Mia, letting her enter first. "I'm just going to put this in the bedroom." She held up her bag and toed off her heals.

"Did you want to get changed?"

She bit her bottom lip as she nodded, fighting back a smile, and wandered down the hall, closing the bedroom door behind her. I went into the kitchen and put on the kettle.

"Tea or coffee?" I called out.

"Coffee would be great," I heard her call out.

I had just set the coffees on the coffee table and stood up when Mia appeared, wearing my favorite little white boy shorts and a tank top. My total sex kitten had changed back into the girl next door, and she looked good enough to eat.

I turned the TV on and turned on the fireplace. "Have a seat. I'm just going to go and change quick." I couldn't help checking her out as she walked past me and took a seat on the couch.

I quickly ran down to the bedroom, changing as fast as I could, and stopped into my home office on the way back out. I grabbed the small box off the shelf and walked back into the living room.

"Happy Valentine's Day." I sat down on the couch beside her and held out a small white box wrapped with a red ribbon.

She looked at me hesitantly, then between me and the box that sat in my hand. "What is that?"

"A little something, nothing big." I met her eyes. "Open it." I held it in front of her, shaking it.

She reached out and took the box from my hand, the tips of her fingers brushing mine.

"You didn't need to do this. I mean the flowers, dinner, they were wonderful."

I smiled and nodded. "I know. Just open it."

She pulled at the ribbon, allowing it to drop into her lap, looked at me, and pulled the lid off the box. I felt the anxiety building in my chest at what lay inside. It had no monetary value, something I had never dared give to Alyssa, but Mia was different. I feared, however, that her answer would crush my heart in an instant. She pulled out the folded piece of paper and opened it, reading the words that I had scrawled on it. Her hand went to her mouth, tears filled her eyes, and she looked up at me.

"I love you too," she whispered, climbing into my lap and wrapping her body around mine.

I kissed her slow and deep, lying down beneath her on the couch and tucked her between me and the back of the couch. I ran my fingers through her hair while looking into her eyes, every now and then kissing her gently, my heart full at her answer.

Chapter Twenty

Bryce

Eight in the morning, and I sat at the boardroom table across from Chase. The view was a far cry from what I had left at home in my bed this morning. I hadn't wanted to leave her as I glanced at her sprawled across my bed sound asleep. Her long, dark hair sprawled across her back, her sexy long leg peeking out of the blanket right up to her thigh, the soft moan that had escaped her lips as I kissed her good-bye. I had wrapped her in blankets and quietly snuck out of the condo with just enough time to spare to grab a coffee.

We had been sitting there for twenty minutes, our client sitting beside me glancing impatiently at his watch as we waited. The receptionist who had brought us to the room finally appeared, carrying a tray of hot coffee and a plate of muffins for everyone.

"I'm sorry for the delay. Mr. Bentley is just waiting on a phone call and he should be right in."

Chase nodded and met my eyes. "I told you something isn't right here."

Mr. Ward, our client, whispered to us both, "Bastard is hiding something."

I took a mug of coffee and a muffin. Even though I felt like a million bucks after spending the last two nights with Mia, I was tired, and I was running low on patience this morning. I wanted to get this meeting over with so that I could get home and spend the evening with her.

"It's okay. We agree with you. Just let us look over the rest of what is presented. There is nothing to worry about. We won't advise you to enter into an agreement if something is amiss," Chase answered, taking a muffin and coffee as well.

I glanced at my watch. We had been sitting there for almost thirty minutes when finally, Dollanger and his sidekick Bentley walked in.

"Gentlemen, good morning," Bentley said, dropping a stack of papers on the table. "Now I have some of the reports, but I'm just waiting for the rest. Apparently, there is a bit of traffic and the department head is running late."

I glanced to Chase who looked back at me.

Bentley didn't wait. He dug right into the files in front of him, handing them to Ward, who handed them over to Chase and me. We started going over things as Bentley droned on in the background, trying to explain things to us.

I made a mental note of the questions I wanted to ask as he continued spewing information at both of us. I pulled out my legal pad and pen and started marking things down as I went over the documents in front of me.

A knock at the door pulled my attention away from what I was writing. "Sorry to interrupt, Mark, Mr. Dollanger, sir, but there is someone here to see you."

She didn't have time to announce anything else before Hunter walked in, and when he stepped off to the side, Mia came in behind him. What the hell? This was where she worked? Her eyes fell to mine, and she quickly turned her face away from me, first in embarrassment, and then a flash of surprise, then hurt mixed with anger flooding it.

Please tell me Mia didn't work for this company. If so, there was way more amiss here than we thought.

"Mia, care to disclose what you have told me?" Hunter asked, waiting for her to take the floor. She kept her eyes on the floor, her cheeks going red every time her eyes would meet mine.

I kept my attention on her, my head held high. I hadn't been prouder of her than I was at this very moment, even if this was her employer. She had decided to take control and stand up for herself.

"Gentlemen," her soft voice called out, "before you pursue this agreement, you should know that these reports have been doctored."

Ward looked to me and Chase, his eyes giving away everything he had been wondering.

"Whoa, wait a minute, Mia, you shouldn't make such accusations," Mark said, placing his hand on his shoulder. "Please excuse us for a moment. Mia has been very stressed lately, and she has recently gone off on sick leave."

Mia started shaking her head, but he grabbed her by the shoulders and turned her away from us.

"Bentley, let the lady speak," I announced to the room. "We are interested in whatever she has to say. Mia, is it? Please go ahead." I wasn't going to allow her to be shuffled off. I knew the things she had to say mattered.

She shrugged Mark off her. "The reports have been doctored by me, under the direction of Mark," she said, looking to Hunter. He stood back and nodded his head.

Bentley looked at her then to Hunter, clenching his jaw tight, his head about ready to explode. He let out a nervous laugh. "She doesn't know what she is talking about," he lied.

"I can prove it," she said, looking over to me, and once again quickly avoiding my eyes.

"Mark," Dollanger questioned, "what is she talking about?"

Mark looked at me, fire burning in his eyes. I knew he was buried. He couldn't get out of this.

"Here." She handed Chase a bunch of documents. "These are the real documents. You can see from the date on the bottom of them. I took copies before I left on vacation, and while I was gone, I ended up getting fired. He asked me to fudge the reports before I left and threatened my job. I did what he asked, but I took copies of the correct ones."

Chase opened the files and looked at all the statements. "Everything here is showing a major, major loss," he said, studying them.

Hunter stood back, his arms crossed over his chest, watching everything unfold. "My client also has some employment law issues as well. Dollanger, did you know that my client has not had a vacation in fifteen years until recently? That she has over two thousand hours of vacation time banked?"

"What? Bentley, is this true?"

"She has also put in countless amounts of overtime without compensation, often working weekends and weeknights from home as well."

"She's lying," Mark choked out.

Hunter stood back and looked at him. "I don't believe she is. I have every pay statement for the last three years, plus her most current. She has recorded down her hours in a calendar for the past three years. I have gone over her overtime hours and every paystub for the past three years, and they only show payments of a straight forty hours per week. Still care to tell me she is lying?" Hunter asked.

Ward stood up, clearing his throat and taking his jacket from the back of the chair. Chase, Bryce, I don't think we need to spend any more time on this. We are done. I refuse to purchase a company that would treat its employees this way, not to mention I have no idea what it is I am even buying at this point."

Ward nodded his head at Mia and Hunter and excused himself from the room. I could tell Mia didn't know what to say when Ward stepped back into the room.

"Mia, if you would like to come in for an interview, my company is hiring a specialist right in your field. I would be more than happy to employ someone so hard working and loyal as yourself. Here is my card. Call my secretary and set up a meeting." He nodded and left the room.

Mia stood there, her mouth open at what had just transpired.

"Mia, how dare you? You have stolen company property," Mark said, his expression contorting into rage.

"As a matter of fact, my client—"

Mia held her hand up and signaled for Hunter to give

her a second. She swallowed hard and took a deep breath before continuing.

"Actually, no, I didn't. I was doing what you always told me to do from the beginning, and that was cover my ass."

Hunter stepped in behind her. "My client expects to be paid out all two thousand hours of vacation, and we will also be sending in an offer to settle up all overtime hours owed. I will send over a fax of our offer later this week to you, Dollanger. We will expect it to be cleared up within the next couple of weeks. Don't make us drag you into court. Mia, after you." Hunter held his hand out to guide her through the door.

I watched them walk out, a part of me rejoicing inside and wishing I could wrap her in my arms and congratulate her. I had never been prouder of anyone, watching her take control and stand up for herself had turned me on.

"Excuse me for a moment," I said, leaving the room and following Mia and Hunter.

I took the elevator down to the main floor and made my way through the lobby, turning the corner to the front door where I saw Mia standing talking with Hunter. Her hand was over her mouth and she looked as if she was crying, his hand on her shoulder doing his best to comfort her.

Chapter Twenty-One

Mia

I had never been so glad to leave a room in my life. With my heart beating hard and fast in my chest the entire time, I had gone through that whole confrontation, all while Bryce sat across from me. What the hell was he even doing there? Was this the big meeting he had told me about?

Walking down the hall, I picked up my pace. I needed air. I had a million thoughts running through my mind and none of them were good. By the time I hit the lobby, I was almost running, Hunter picking up pace behind me.

"Mia, Mia..." His hand gripped my arm, stopping me. "Mia, what is wrong? Everything went exactly as we hoped it would." Hunter pulled me over to the side into a quiet little corner in the lobby.

"Hunter, I don't care about that." I sniffled.

"Then what is it?"

"Did he know?" I blurted out, looking him in the eyes.

"Did who know?"

"Did Bryce know I worked here? Is that why he picked me up in the airport, to gain insight into this failing company?"

"Mia, wait a minute."

I heard Bryce call out, and I glanced over my shoulder to see him approaching us.

"Don't walk away from him, Mia, talk to him. You need to tell him what you are thinking."

"I've got to go. I can't do this today." I turned and headed toward the main doors, leaving Hunter standing there. I didn't want to be put into a corner, especially one I certainly didn't want to be in. I didn't want to hear what he had to say. I didn't want it to be true, but somewhere in my gut, I was petrified that it was.

"Mia, wait." I felt Bryce grab hold of my arm and spin me around. "Why are you rushing away from me.

"Mia, I'm going to leave the two of you alone. You have a lot to talk about," Hunter said, rubbing my upper arm. "Call me this afternoon. I want to go over the offer before I send it, okay?" He nodded at Bryce and walked out of the building.

"Mia, what is wrong?" Bryce tried to take hold of my hands, but I pulled them away.

"First, I want to thank you for everything, Bryce. I really can't thank you enough." I sniffled and wiped the tears from under my eyes. I had to say good-bye in the fastest way possible. I couldn't stand to hear the truth, and if he just let me leave after this, then we would be good. I would do what I always did: disappear into my busy life. Only right now, there was no busy.

"You're welcome, but why the tears?"

"Did you seek me out?"

He frowned. "What? What are you talking about?"

I huffed, trying to regain control over my emotions. "I guess I'm supposed to believe that it's just a coincidence that you were dealing with the merger for the company that I worked for?"

"Of course, it is, Mia. I don't know what you are talking about."

"The airport, the week at the lake house, you sought me out. Why? Was it just to get information on this company that you didn't have? You needed more dirt, and you knew I worked here, so you sought me out? There is no way I can believe that it's just a coincidence that after all this time I just so happen to run into you."

"Mia, what are you saying?"

"You expect me to believe that all of this is something more?"

Bryce stood there, thinking through my accusations. "What, you think the only reason I got involved with you was to gain inside knowledge about this company? Mia, I'm in love with you."

The tears poured freely down my cheeks as I stood there looking at him, the hurt in his eyes literally ripping my heart from my chest.

"You think I was faking it with you?" he went on. "You think all of this has been some sort of game?"

I slowly nodded my head, wiping more tears from my cheeks. He stood there looking at me, not saying anything for quite a while. He didn't try to comfort me when I thought he would. Instead he came out with an accusation all his own. "Okay, you want to play it that way, then perhaps this is your way of getting back at me?" he stated.

"What?" I said, looking up at him through blurry eyes.

"For that night all those years ago? Maybe you are the one who is playing games with me, Mia. Perhaps you saw me in the airport and figured this would be as good a time as any to get back at me for that night at the party."

"You're serious right now?" I spat.

His eyes drilled into mine. I could see the hurt. I could see that he wasn't lying when he said what I assumed wasn't true. I could also see that what he was saying sounded just as ridiculous as what I was saying.

"Sounds pretty ridiculous, doesn't it?" His sharp look beat down on me.

"Don't bother coming by tonight. I don't want to see you." I looked up into those baby blues and turned and ran out the front door, jutting out into traffic, car tires screeching and horns blaring as I ran across the street to where I was parked. I jumped into my car and pulled away from the curb, another horn blaring from the car I cut off.

I drove aimlessly around the city for a while, not really knowing where to go. I finally stopped at the grocery store, wandering the aisles and throwing food I normally would never eat into the cart, then paid and made my way home. I lugged all the groceries into the house, dropping everything down onto the kitchen floor, when my cell phone rang. Don's name flashed across the screen.

What the hell does he want? I thought to myself. "What?" I barked into the phone.

"Mia, is that you?"

"Who else would it be?" I demanded, pulling some of the items from one of the bags and putting them into the fridge.

"I just thought I would call and let you know I just sent some of your things through FedEx. They were things that you had left here on your last visit. They should arrive sometime in the next couple of days. If not, let me know, and I will call FedEx."

I didn't say anything. I stopped what I was doing and slid down to the floor. My stomach hurt, my head pounded, and I just wanted everything and everyone to leave me alone. I didn't hang up. Instead I sat there, my hand over my eyes, and whispered, "Don, can I ask you something?"

The line was quiet. "Sure." Only I didn't say anything; I just sat there afraid of his answer. "Mia, is everything all right?"

Even though we may not have been right for one another, Don was always one who was able to tell me the truth, even when I didn't want to hear it for myself. He could always pick up on when I was off my game.

"What is so undesirable about me?"

"What do you mean? Nothing is undesirable about you. You're a beautiful person."

"Then why did you not want to be with me?"

I heard him let out a sigh. "Mia it's not that I didn't want to be with you. I did. I tried tirelessly to make things work between us, but you don't trust. You never let anyone close enough to you to ever possibly let someone love you. It took me two years to break down your walls, and if we were apart for more than six months at a time, then I had to do it all over again. It was exhausting. You were constantly finding reasons to push me away, just like you do with everyone."

He was right, he had pegged me perfectly. Thinking back, I had done it with every boyfriend, every friend, and even my own brother. I was the one pushing everyone away.

Even though Don was still talking, I hung up the phone, letting it fall to the floor. I had made a mess of things once again, only this time it was with someone that I truly wanted to have in my life.

I pulled my knees into my chest and wrapped my arms around my legs, burying my face into my lap, trying to figure out how the hell I was going to fix us.

Chapter Twenty-Two

Bryce

I had work that needed to be completed, so I returned to the office after my encounter with Mia. I worked until 6:00 p.m., for as long as I could, until my mind was fully consumed with thoughts of her and how I was going to fix this, how I was going to fix *us*.

I took a long shower when I got home, trying to let go of some of the stress I was carrying. I had planned on coming home, making dinner, having a few drinks, and going to bed, since she didn't want to see me. Those words had hurt, and for part of the afternoon, I considered just giving up and letting her go, but my heart had other ideas.

I needed to see her, I needed to fix this with us, and truthfully, I didn't want to lose her.

It sounded ridiculous, even to me. It may have only been a couple of weeks, but those couple of weeks had been the best of my life.

I changed into a pair of jeans and a sweater, grabbed a water from the fridge, and headed out the door.

I drove the long way through town, making one stop on my way: my buddy's jewelry store. I wasn't in a rush. I was sure she would be up late tonight making her favorite stress meal anyway: meatballs and cookies. I spent a good hour in the store with my friend trying to find the perfect item, and after finding the only thing that spoke to me, I left armed with the little white box wrapped in red ribbon.

I continued driving through town, thinking of what I was going to say, when I finally came face-to-face with her. Should I just give her the box? No that was what I would have done with Alyssa. Perhaps I should just talk to her first. Whichever way I decided to do it, I was sure she would find something wrong with it and probably kick me to the curb. I had been so unfair to her this afternoon with my accusations.

Twenty minutes later, I pulled into Mia's driveway. I cut the engine and sat there for ten minutes just staring at the house. The light was on in the living room, and I could see flashes of light from the TV reflecting against the curtains.

I sat there until I saw her through the curtains, carrying a plate in her hands across the front room where she must have sat down on the couch.

I couldn't sit out here forever, so I opened the car door and stepped out into the cold night, the remains of the last snowfall crunching under my feet.

I shoved the little box into my jacket pocket and knocked on the door. Seconds later, the outside light was turned on and my nerves went into overdrive. The inside door pulled open, and Mia stood there. She didn't move to open the inside door and invite me in. Instead she looked at me through the glass. How I wanted to wrap her in my arms and make everything go away.

"Could I come in?"

Surprisingly she didn't argue or tell me no. Instead she stepped to the side and opened the door for me. She shut and locked the door behind me and held her hand out for my coat, still not saying a word. After she hung that up, I followed her as she walked into the kitchen carrying her empty plate. There on the counter sat a tray of meatballs, and I could smell the sweetness of her chocolate chip cookies that must have been cooking in the oven.

A small smile came to my lips.

"What's so funny?" she asked, squinting at me, a serious expression on her face.

"Nothing, it's just I didn't rush over here because I

figured this was what you would be doing," I said, pointing to the tray of meatballs.

"Want one?" she asked, holding the tray up to me.

I took one, the oven timer letting out a loud beep. She set the tray back down and opened the oven door, pulling out a tray of chocolate chip cookies.

She pulled another plate down from the cupboard and loaded some meatballs and cookies onto it then held it out for me to take. "Dinner?"

I smiled, taking the plate from her, only she didn't smile back. Instead she picked up her plate, shoved past me, and went into the living room.

I took in a deep breath. This was going to be a long night. I followed her into the living room and sat down on the couch beside her. She adjusted herself so her body turned into mine. Bending off a piece of the warm cookie, she popped it into her mouth.

Nothing was said between the two of us while we ate, but I could feel the tension in the room. I finished my food first and set my empty plate on the table in front of us.

"I'm sorry..." We both said in unison.

I couldn't take it anymore. The thought of her being angry with me for saying something as stupid as I had was killing me.

"I wasn't being fair to you," she mumbled. "I thought about it once I left. I panicked when I saw you sitting there, staring back at me." A single tear escaped her eye. "I was so afraid that you were only after the information on the company and all we had shared wasn't real that it was all I could do to remain in the room."

"Wasn't real? You think I could fake that, fake any of it?"

"You're a guy. Of course, you can. Sex to you is all the same, whether it comes with feelings or not." She laughed and rolled her eyes.

"That isn't true Mia. Maybe once I could, but never more than that, and never in my entire life have I told a woman I loved them when I haven't. And if you seriously think I could do that, then you don't know me at all," I said pointedly.

"Bryce I—"

I stood up and went to grab my jacket from the closet.

"You're leaving? Fine, just go, Bryce," she choked out.

I pulled my coat off the hanger and searched the pockets, finally pulling the little box out, and then hung my jacket on the handle. I walked back over and sat down beside her without saying a word.

"Mia I'm sorry too. I was out of line when I said what I said to you about you getting back at me. I was hurt and thought it was easiest to cover it up by lashing out at you." I held the box out to her, and her eyes traveled to my hands. "Take it," I whispered.

She cautiously reached out and took the box from my

hand, her fingers grazing mine, instantly sending a wave of heat through me. I watched her tear-streaked face as she slowly pulled at the ribbon. Untying it, she lifted the lid off the box. The tears then started to pour, as soon as she looked at what was inside, and she put the lid back over top of it.

"What is it? Don't you like it?" I asked.

"It's not that. I love it."

"Then what is it?" I asked, placing two fingers under her chin and pulling her head in my direction so she would look at me.

"It's just, I was so unfair to you about that comment I made today. I'm a master at pushing people away. I spoke to Don today and asked him what was so undesirable about me. That was his answer. I'm scared. I don't want to lose you, but my instinct is telling me to push you away from me." She sniffled.

"Well, then I guess it's a good thing that us Malone boys don't give up that easy, isn't it? I'm not going anywhere, Mia. My heart belongs to you. You are my home." I moved closer to her and pulled her into my arms.

"How can you possibly know that? It's only been—"

"I know...it's only been a couple of weeks. Actually, that isn't true. It's been years, Mia. Years of wanting you," I said, the back of my hand brushing against her cheek. "It just took seeing you again to realize it. Out of sight, out of mind is true, but when your heart holds feelings for someone, it kindly reminds you not to give up so easily. So, I'm not going to stop until I get it."

She buried her face into my neck and let out a sob. We sat together for a while, her head resting on my shoulder. Once she had calmed down, I kissed her forehead and took the little box off her lap, opening it. I removed the white gold chain that held the little infinity charm.

"Sit forward and hold your hair up."

She did as I asked, and I placed the chain around her neck.

"This was the only thing there that spoke to me. It represents how long and how much I finally realized that I loved you," I whispered into her ear and kissed the side of her neck, inching toward the top of her shoulder.

She shut the TV off and took my hand in hers, pulling me up. The sexy playfulness in her eyes nearly sent me to my knees as she led me down the hall toward her bedroom. With each step, she shed an article of clothing—first her socks, then her pants, next her shirt, until she stood in front of her bedroom door in nothing but a black lace bra and panties and the necklace I had bought her. I went to step forward to kiss her, but she placed her hand on my chest and stepped into her bedroom.

Grabbing my sweater, I pulled it over my head and undid the button on my jeans, a loud clinking sound as my belt hit her hardwood floors. I took a step forward while she took a step back, until she had fallen back onto the bed.

I ripped the cups of her bra down, exposing her breasts to me, and sucked her one nipple into my mouth while rolling the other between my finger and thumb. Mia instantly inhaled and let out a moan as her back lifted off the bed. I left her breasts and ran my hand down the center of her stomach to the waist of her panties, and in once swift pull, I ripped them from her body. She let out a gasp.

"Bryce, those were my favorite..."

"Shhhh, I will get you more."

She giggled as I placed a hand on each of her knees, pushing her legs open. As I looked down, I could see she was already soaked. I looked back up to see her lust-filled eyes watching me. I kept watching her as I ran my fingers through her wetness and up over her clit. Her eyes closed and she let out a soft moan. I pushed my boxers down, my cock already hard and throbbing. I needed inside of her right now.

"Where do you keep the condoms?" I asked, praying that she had some.

She bit her lower lip and shook her head no. "No condom," she whispered. "I want to feel you."

"You sure?" I kneeled between her legs.

She nodded her head, her sex-filled eyes looking up at me. I leaned down, connecting with her lips, my tongue running through her mouth, tasting her. I grabbed my cock, giving it a couple of pumps, which was totally unnecessary, as hard as I was, and I ran it through her wetness. I pushed inside of her slowly, watching her face as I buried myself deep into her. She was fucking beautiful. I loved watching her as I pulled out and pushed all the way in again. Her hands reaching up behind her head, she gripped the pillow the harder I thrust into her, soft moans escaping her lips.

"Rub your clit for me," I demanded. "Show me how you make yourself come."

She shook her head, a soft blush coming over her already heated cheeks.

I sat back on my heels; my cock fully planted inside of her. "Show me." I took hold of her hand and placed it on her lower belly. "Rub yourself," I whispered.

I could tell she was hesitant at first, but then her hand slowly moved to her center and she started rubbing her clit. I felt like I could bust, watching her pleasure herself while my cock was buried inside of her. I was fighting to hold back my own orgasm just watching her, but then I felt her tighten around me, and the sound of her moans getting louder and louder the closer she came, it was almost impossible, and as soon as I felt the hot rush of heat from her, I too let myself go, filling her full.

We lay in bed, her head on my chest, her body wrapped around mine, fitting perfectly against me, as if it was the only one that belonged there. We were on the cusp of sleep after our third round. I pulled her closer and she let out a sleepy, sexy little moan.

"Don't push me away anymore," I whispered.

She opened her sleepy eyes and looked up at me. "I won't. Well, I will try not to." She placed a little kiss on my chest and put her head back down.

"Good, now I don't want to scare you but move in with me."

I could tell, as soon as those words were past my lips, that she was scared and almost ready to bolt right out of the bed the way her body stiffened. I started rubbing her arm, and I felt her start to relax.

"Move in with me," I repeated, kissing her forehead. "We'll take it slow."

She nodded her head against my chest, and I heard her sniffle.

Chapter Twenty-Three

Bryce - Nine months later

It was almost 8:00 p.m. and I was still sitting behind my desk at the office. The day had been long, and I couldn't wait to get out of here tonight. Mia had finally agreed to move in with me, and she was finally settled into my condo. We were putting her house up on the market this weekend.

I sat back in my chair and opened my desk drawer. My eyes instantly fell to the little black velvet box that had been sitting there since last week. I couldn't put it off any longer. I needed to make that call before I left the office tonight.

I scrolled through my contact list in search of Grant's

number. It had been about a year since I had last spoken to him, right when things with Alyssa had gone south. Before dialing, I pulled open my bottom drawer and picked up the bottle of scotch that was hidden there, pouring myself a shot. I had done the same thing before the last phone call, only this time it was for an entirely different reason. I downed that shot and poured a half shot more, knowing after this call I had to drive home, then I picked up the phone and dialed his number.

The phone rang and rang, and just when I thought I might be off the hook, I heard his voice. "Dr. Hollis."

"Grant?" I said into the phone.

"You've got him. Who's this?" he asked, sounding a little confused. No doubt he was busy and was probably still at the hospital.

"It's Bryce," I answered, rotating that little velvet box between my fingers.

"One second." I heard him ramble off a long list of orders to someone and then finally silence.

"Did I catch you at a bad time?" I asked, kind of praying he said yes.

"No, not at all. Sorry, just at the hospital. I was just about to head out on lunch anyways. How the fuck are you?" He chuckled into the phone.

"Good, great actually. Work has been steady, and I finally made partner."

"That's fantastic, man! Congratulations."

"Thanks! Yeah, my brothers always make Chase and I earn everything, those bastards." We both laughed.

"How's Mia doing? She told me you two finally moved in together."

"Yeah, she finally agreed. It took some convincing on my part. She moved in with me earlier this month finally, and we are putting her house on the market."

"I'm glad to hear that. She seems really happy, far cry from one of the last few times I spoke with her."

We spent the better half of the next fifteen minutes catching up. Grant told me about his wife and kids, sharing with me that he was up for another promotion at the hospital. He had worked hard and made a good life for himself.

"Listen, if you guys are able to soon, why don't you both make the trip out here. It would be great to see you both. It's been a while, and Mia still hasn't met the kids."

"Sounds like a great idea. Send me your holidays, and I will make sure we get out there."

I heard Grant being paged in the background.

"Shit, man, I've got to go. My hour is almost up."

I could hear him chug down whatever it was he was drinking.

I sat there, still turning the little black velvet box in my hand. The purpose for my call quickly coming back to me. "Listen, can I ask you something."

I heard the page go off again in the background.

"Give me one minute."

I sat there listening as he spoke to someone in the background. I drank down the mouthful of scotch I had poured myself, feeling that good old burning sensation as I swallowed the golden liquid.

He gave out orders, finally returning to our call. "Sorry about that. It's not an emergency, thank God, but I do need to get going. What's up?"

I kept turning that little black box between my fingers, trying to find the courage for my call. "Grant, I called because, well, you are Mia's only family, and I..."

"You want to ask her to marry you, don't you?" he said, taking the words right from my mouth that otherwise may never have made it out.

I let out the breath I was holding. "Yes, I do. I want to spend the rest of my life with her."

"Then go for it, man. Let me know how it goes, and I swear if she doesn't say yes, ship her out to me for a couple of weeks and I will change her mind for you."

We both laughed. It was good to know that after all these years, Grant still had my back.

"Thanks, man. I'll talk to you soon."

We hung up the phone and I sat there for a couple of minutes still twirling that little black box in my hands. Now I just needed to find the perfect time to ask her.

I tucked the box into my jacket pocket and gathered my things, finally shutting off the light to my office.

The drive home was quick, and I took the elevator up to the condo. When I opened the door, soft music filled the apartment, the lights were dimmed in the living room, and a candle was burning on the coffee table.

I dropped my briefcase just inside the door and put my keys on the table. Mia had already begun to make changes, adding her feminine touch to things in the short time she had lived with me.

I could hear the shower running and quietly walked toward our bedroom, but first I slipped into my office and placed the little black velvet box at the back of the center drawer where Mia wouldn't find it.

I undressed and slipped into the bathroom. Steam filled the room, but I could see the outline of Mia standing in the shower, her back turned to me.

"Hey, sexy. I'm home." I pulled the shower door open and stepped inside, Mia turning to face me, my eyes washing over her perfect, full breasts, my cock instantly going hard at the sight. I hadn't been able to keep my hands off her, especially when she stood there looking at me so innocently. I pulled her warm body against mine and kissed the side of her neck, breathing in her clean scent.

"I'm so glad to see you." She wrapped her arms around my neck, meeting my lips.

"Did you get everything done at the house with Autumn?" I asked.

"Yep, it's all done and ready for the real estate agent tomorrow. He's hoping for a fast sale."

"Good, then we don't have to go back tonight?" I grabbed her under the ass and picked her up, she wrapped her legs around my waist, and I backed her up until she was resting against the tile, attacking her mouth again.

"Bryce, put me down." She laughed as I kissed my way down her neck and across her collarbone.

"No way. You're mine!" I buried my face in the side of her neck, causing her to laugh out loud. I slowly put her down and smacked her ass and pulled her in for a long kiss.

"Are you hungry?" she asked as she pulled those beautiful soft lips from mine, the look in her eyes screaming for me to take her right there.

"Starving."

"Well, clean yourself up. I'll go and make us something to eat."

She let go of my hand and went to open the shower door, but I pulled her back against my chest, my arm instantly securing around her waist, the other hand grasping her breast. As my fingers brushed over her nipple, I heard a little whimper escape her mouth, and I bit her earlobe, causing her to drop her head to my shoulder as my other hand traveled down between her legs, my fingers making contact with her clit.

"You're so bad," she breathed out, parting her legs just a little.

"You love it," I whispered.

Twenty minutes later, Mia left the shower fully sated and wrapped in a large black towel, leaving me to quickly shower. "I'll go make us something to eat," she called out, leaving the bathroom.

I had changed into my lounge pants and T-shirt and wandered into my office. I pulled open the center drawer and reached to the back, pulling out the little black box and putting it into my pocket. I heard Mia banging around in the kitchen, and my stomach let out a loud grumble at the thought of food.

I rounded the corner and noticed she had turned the fireplace on. A bottle of wine sat in the chiller in the living room beside two empty glasses, and a plate of cheese and crackers sat beside it.

"It will just be a minute. I have brie in the oven," she said, smiling over at me.

"No problem." I walked over, poured the wine, and then went to look out the window. I wrapped my hand around the little black velvet box that sat in my pocket as I watched Mia's reflection in the glass. Just when I thought

I had enough courage to turn and ask her, she walked into the room carrying the plate of hot brie.

"Did you want to watch a movie or something?" she asked, sitting down on the edge of the couch.

I shook my head. I just wanted to ask her. I wouldn't be able to eat if I didn't, my nerves getting the better of me.

"Are you going to come and sit down?" she asked, looking up at me, a worried expression coming over her face.

"Can you come here?" I asked.

"Bryce, what is the matter with you?" she asked. Concern now lined her face as she stood up and came over to me. "Is everything okay?" she asked as she got close enough to run her hand over my shoulder.

I didn't answer her. Instead I dropped to my knee.

"Bryce, what are you..."

Her words stopped as soon as she saw what I held in my hand, her eyes growing wide. The last thing I wanted to do was scare her. We had been in such a great place over the last eight months, I didn't want her to start pushing me away again.

My hands shook as I lifted the lid on that tiny box to produce the custom designed ring I had ordered from the local jeweler. Her hands shook as they covered her mouth.

"Mia, these last few months with you have been amazing." She held her hand up to stop me, but I kept going. "I can't ever imagine my life without you in it again. I want you to be my wife." I looked up into her eyes as they filled with tears and instantly, I became afraid she was going to curl back up into the person she used to be.

She surprised me, and instead she slowly reached down and took my hand in hers and nodded her head. I had never ripped anything from a package so fast as I did that ring and placed it on her finger.

Forgetting about the food or how hungry I was, I picked her up, her legs instantly wrapping around my waist, and I carried her down the hall.

"I want to see you in nothing but that ring, moaning my fucking name," I murmured into her ear as I lowered her to the floor.

Chapter Twenty-Four

Mia

I watched from the front window as Bryce and the real estate agent walked down to the edge of the lawn and hung the sold sign. At first, we were going to keep my little bungalow, but then we decided we didn't want to have to deal with renters.

I looked around the little bungalow where I had spent the better part of my life, reminiscing about all the events that had taken place while I had lived here. This house held so many memories for me, all of them flashing before my eyes like an old movie.

I heard the backdoor slam and ran my fingers under my eyes to remove any tears that may have fallen. I didn't want Bryce to think I wasn't happy with our decision. The truth was I couldn't be happier. It was just hard to let go of certain things.

"Mia?" I heard him call out.

"Yeah, I'm in here," I called back from the front room, still looking out the front window.

"There you are. You just about ready? We are supposed to meet everyone down at the little cafe by the water."

I bit my lower lip and looked around the room one last time. "I think so." I couldn't help a twinge of sadness hitting my voice. It was harder to say good-bye to these memories than I thought it was going to be, but my future held so many more in store for me, and I couldn't wait to embark on the journey with Bryce.

"How about we go and take a walk down by the water?" he said, wrapping his arms around me from behind and kissing me gently on the cheek. "Just us, before we meet up with everyone. I'll call and tell them we're running late and bump the time up to eight."

"That would be nice. I would like that," I said, leaning back into him, letting his warmth and strong embrace envelop me for a second.

"All right then, let's go." Placing another kiss on my cheek, he grabbed my hand, but I was hesitant and didn't move.

"Could you maybe give me a minute?" I asked, looking

into his eyes and swallowing hard. "I just need a minute or two."

"Of course. I will be out in the car, okay? Come out when you're ready." He leaned in and kissed me before opening the front door.

I watched him walk down the walkway and get into the car. I didn't think saying good-bye to this house would be this hard. I took my time going through each room of the house, reflecting over the last fifteen years of my life once more. I remembered the first night I had gotten the key. I had come over and just sat in the living room on the floor for hours, so excited about what the future held for me here. But now I had such bigger and better things to look forward to.

I glanced at my watch, realizing that Bryce had been sitting waiting for me for close to twenty minutes, and walked to the front door and pulled it open. Taking one final look around, I walked out the door, locking it behind me. I handed the key to the real estate agent who stood beside his car, thanked him for everything, and climbed into Bryce's car.

"You okay?" he asked, putting his phone down on the console between the seats.

"Yep. Let's go," I whispered. He backed out of the driveway, and for the final time, I looked back at the dark house.

It was a quiet ride as Bryce drove down to the waterfront. I looked out the window, watching the trees pass by, listening to the soft music Bryce had playing in the car. I was lost in my thoughts when I felt his hand on mine. He didn't say anything. He just held it tight for the remainder of the drive.

Once we arrived downtown, it was a matter of seconds before we found a parking spot. He came around the car and pulled my door open, offering me his hand. "Did you want a coffee first?"

"That would be great. Was everyone okay with waiting until eight?" I asked as I climbed out of the car.

"Of course. It's all good." He winked at me.

Once we had our coffee, we started walking around the water. It was a gorgeous night, a cool breeze off the lake blowing around us. It was only the end of September, and a few boats from the marina were out on the water, the people enjoying one of the last boat rides of the season.

We continued to walk for a bit, finally sitting down on a little bench halfway around the lake.

"I was thinking, with the money from the sale of the house and my settlement, what if we put that towards a down payment on a house?"

Bryce was quiet, looking off in the distance of the water. I was a little scared when he didn't answer me right away.

"Bryce? Did you hear me?"

"Yeah."

He seemed so far away, I could sense my insecurities rising again and the absolute fear to push away and I had to ask him. "Bryce, have we...have we made a mistake?"

"What?" That had gotten his attention. "No, love, what would make you think that? I was just thinking about where we would move to and about the wedding. You are the furthest thing from a mistake. Don't ever think that." He looked into my eyes and wrapped his arm around me, pulling me in closer. "I seriously cannot wait until I see you walk down that aisle in a white dress, looking all perfect, just so I can rip it off you later and make you scream my name."

We both laughed, my nerves instantly calming.

"And I think it's a great idea to do with the money, but I don't want to rush into something. Let's wait until we find the perfect place."

We finished our coffees, watching the boats out on the water, and then made our way over to the cafe. We had yet to tell anyone about the engagement and really wanted everyone in one place all together.

As we approached the cafe, we both noticed Hunter and Carter's cars parked out front.

"Looks like everyone is here already," Bryce said, pulling the door open for me and guiding me in, his hand resting on my lower back.

As soon as I walked in, I was met with a huge congratulations sign and balloons everywhere. Hope and

Autumn came rushing over to me and reached for my hand. "Let us see," they squealed in delight.

I glanced over my shoulder at Bryce who held his hands up in an innocent gesture. "My brothers knew. I had to tell them what your answer was." He shrugged his shoulders and chuckled.

Soon Bryce was seated over with Carter, Hunter, and Chase discussing work, while I sat with Autumn and Hope looking over wedding dress designs on our phones. The plans were already starting, and I couldn't think of two better people to help me plan my wedding.

I felt a puff of air against my legs as someone entered the cafe, and as I went to turn, Autumn grabbed my attention to share with me a dress she thought would look perfect on me, when suddenly I felt someone's hands over my eyes, the room going dark.

"All right, very funny, Bryce. What other kinds of surprises do you have up your sleeve now?" I said, pulling at his hands.

I blinked, letting my eyes adjust once again to the light, and turned around, expecting to see Bryce standing there with some goofy smile on his face, only it wasn't Bryce, and I kind of felt lightheaded at who was standing in front of me.

"You look like you've seen a ghost, Mia. What the hell. Aren't you excited to see your own brother?" Grant asked, standing in front of me, June and the kids standing behind him.

My eyes got blurry as the tears built up in them, and I wrapped my arms around my brother. I had never thought I meant that much to Grant until he stood here in front of me. He had carted the whole family across the states just to be here to celebrate our engagement.

Everyone was quiet as we stood there, me crying into my brother's chest, him hugging me tighter than I ever remembered.

"I wouldn't have missed this for the world. When Bryce called and asked us to be here tonight, we couldn't say no. You mean more to me than you will ever know," he whispered in my ear.

A deep sob escaped my chest as I held him tighter. "Thank you so much for coming."

"All right, you two, break it up. If you weren't related, I'd swear you were trying to steal my woman," Bryce said, getting up and shaking his hand, everyone laughing.

I finally grew quiet, looking around the table at everyone. It was the first time we had all been together in years, and it finally truly felt like home. I had found my place. I had just been lost for the past fifteen years, trying to find my way back to where I belonged.

I quietly excused myself from the table and headed toward the washroom. When I was on my way back to the table, I felt someone grab me from behind and pull me back into them.

Bryce wrapped his arms around me and kissed my cheek. "Were you surprised?"

I looked over to where everyone sat and nodded my head. "You did this?" I asked.

"I did. We've been talking for a bit now. We have been planning this since the night I called and asked him for your hand," he whispered, kissing the edge of my ear.

"You asked my brother?" I asked.

"I did. I figured it was only the proper thing to do. I mean, you don't know where your father is, and your mother, God rest her soul, is gone. He was the next logical choice. I told him when I was planning it, and he promised me he would be here to celebrate."

I looked up into my future husband's eyes, and for the first time in my life, I had never been so sure of anything.

<h1 align="center">Chapter Twenty-Five</h1>

Mia - Epilogue

We lay together on the couch, the fire burning and soft music filling the room. Outside, the winter storm raged on, covering everything with snow.

I giggled. "Doesn't this remind you of the first time we were here?" I asked. We had decided to spend our two-week honeymoon at the lake house, and just like the first time, the day before we were to leave to return home, snow decided to fall, trapping us here.

"Yeah, it does. I guess that is fate's way of telling us our honeymoon isn't quite over yet." He laughed, kissing me. He pulled away when we heard a gust of wind outside.

"It's getting pretty wild out. I should probably bring in a bit more wood, sweetie," Bryce said, removing his arm from under me and sitting up. "I'll be right back. I don't want to have to fight my way through all that later." He grabbed his hoodie from the couch and threw it over his head.

I watched him go and pulled the blanket around my body. Even though it was warm inside, I was cold without him. He brought in three armfuls of wood and dropped them in the wood box, filling it, and threw another log on the fire before returning to my side.

"You barely touched your wine. You all right?"

"Yeah. My stomach is a little upset tonight," I answered, getting comfortable again as he slid in beside me. "Cold out there?"

"It's more than cold. I would suggest the hot tub, but I think we might freeze," he said, kissing my forehead.

"It's okay, I'm exhausted," I said, yawning. "Did you want to go to bed."

Bryce laughed out loud. "Babe you don't need to ask me twice," he said, wiggling his eyebrows at me. "I could use a little stress relief."

"You can always use stress relief." I laughed, kicking the blankets off me.

We had barely made it down the hall and he had already stripped my T-shirt off, leaving it in a pile on the floor in the hallway as he held me in his arms, kissing me hard.

"Fuck me, you are going to be the death of me, woman," he whispered between kisses.

I could already feel him hard against me. He threw open the bedroom door and held me as I walked backward to the bed. He pulled the drawstring on his lounge pants, allowing them to fall to the floor, his hard cock saluting me.

I sat up on the bed, teasing his cock with my tongue as he stood before me. He fisted his hand in my hair as I continued to deliver little licks to the head of his cock, licking the bead of precum off him.

"Fuck. Don't tease me. Take it in your mouth," he hissed.

I looked up at him, my eyes teasing him as I continued with the torturous little licks.

With his free hand, he held onto my breast, rubbing his thumb over my nipple, his touch running a chill through my body. He gently pinched my nipple through the fabric of my bra, causing me to jump. He stopped immediately. "Did I hurt you?"

I shook my head. "Just a little sensitive is all. Slow down," I whispered. Everything about me felt sensitive tonight.

He pushed me gently back, gripping the waist of my

silk pajama pants and pulling them off me, and he crawled in beside me, shutting off the bedside light and pulling the blankets around us. I straddled his waist and felt his hands run up my back and flick the clasp on the back of my bra, his fingers grazing my shoulders as he pulled my bra down and off me, my nipples instantly hardening at the coolness of the room.

Bryce sat up and took one of them in his mouth, sucking and licking. Again, a sharp intake of breath and a jump stopped him. "Baby are you sure you are okay?"

"Yeah, just slow down."

"Come then, lay down." He guided me off him and I lay back into the mattress. He propped himself up on his elbow and met my lips, kissing me slow and positioning himself in between my legs. Kissing me deeply, he slid his way inside of me and started thrusting slow and deep.

Everything about me felt heightened, and within minutes, I could already feel myself getting tighter around him, finally screaming out my orgasm as he emptied himself inside of me.

I lay wrapped in his arms. "You sure you're okay?" he whispered, kissing the side of my neck.

"Yeah, I'm okay." I closed my eyes. We had just gotten married. I wasn't sure how he would react to the news I had to deliver, but I didn't want to wait any longer.

"You remember how I went to see Dr. Price just before we left? I wanted him to renew my birth control."

"Yep, did you remember to pick up your prescription before we left?" he murmured sleepily.

"No."

"No, sweetie, you know how I hate wearing condoms now. Both Hunter and Carter warned me once I went bare, I wouldn't go back." He chuckled.

"Sounds like your brothers." I laughed.

"Well, I don't want to go back," he whined, tickling my side and causing me to wiggle away and scream. "You feel way too good."

"You don't have to," I murmured.

He went quiet, releasing the hold he had on my side. "Mia? What do you mean?" He questioned, raising up on his elbow and turning on the bedside light so he could see me.

I looked up at him, a smile falling on my lips at the questioning look on his face.

"Really? I'm going to be a dad," he whispered.

I was sure I saw a tear in his eye as the words fell from his lips.

I nodded my head without saying anything and bit my lower lip. "I know we talked about it and everything. I know you wanted to wait and travel..."

He placed a single finger up to my lips. "It doesn't matter, baby. Now, next year, never...it doesn't matter. It's going to be an amazing journey, fun and exciting. Get excited, sweetie, we are going to have an amazing adventure together."

The End

Mia's Spicy Meatballs
Makes Approx 40 Meatballs

1 lb Lean Ground Beef

1 lb Italian Sausage (casing removed)

1 cup seasoned bread crumb mix (see recipe below)

½ cup coconut milk

1 egg

1. Mix ground meat and sausage meat together
2. In a separate bowl add 1 cup breadcrumb mix with ½ cup coconut milk and 1 egg, mix together
3. Add wet mixture to meat and mix together well.
4. Preheat oven to 375 degrees on convection roast.
5. Weigh out meat into 1 oz portions and roll into balls.
6. Place meatballs on cookie sheet and lightly spray meatballs with olive oil spray.
7. Roast in oven for 45 mins or until golden brown.
8. Let cool and enjoy!

Mia's Spicy Breadcrumb Mixture
Makes approx. two cups

1 cup breadcrumbs

¼ cup whole wheat flour

¼ cup all purpose flour

2 tsp dried minced onion flakes

1 tbsp oregano

1 tbsp basil

½ tsp paprika

½ tsp chili flakes

½ tsp chipotle chili powder

½ tsp crushed fennel seed

2 tsp granulated garlic

½ tsp marjoram

1 tsp parsley

2 tsp sea salt

2 tsp black ground pepper

Combine all ingredients into a bowl and mix. Store leftover mixture in airtight container.

Sophie

The heat from the morning sun was hot as I made my way down the street to Aroma Mocha. I was on my way to meet Jenna for our usual Saturday morning coffee date." Normally, we walked to Aroma Mocha together after our yoga class, but she couldn't make it this morning. Instead, I made my way to the local cafe and flung my mat under my arm as I pulled the door open and stepped into the amazing smell of roasted coffee beans and freshly baked cinnamon buns. I looked around the dining area for Jenna, and when I didn't see her, I made my way to the counter and placed our usual order, then took a seat in our usual booth. I pulled my cell phone from my yoga bag and quickly checked my messages. I had just finished replying to someone at work when I spotted Jenna entering the small cafe. She spotted me right away and waved as she made her way through the crowd, her cell phone pressed up against her ear.

"I'm sorry, just a second. It's Matt," she mouthed as she pointed to her phone.

I smiled and slid out of my jacket while waiting for my vanilla latte and blueberry muffin to be delivered. I tried not to pay attention to Jenna while she spoke to Matt, but it was impossible. My best friend looked so happy, and I loved how her face lit up as she listened to whatever it was Matt was saying. The excitement in her voice was almost contagious when she responded to him. I wondered what it was like to be as happy as Jenna was. I hadn't had a decent relationship in years—well, honestly, never, but who was counting.

Jenna beamed as she hung up the phone and tucked it into her purse and turned her attention towards me. "Good morning," she sang. "How was yoga?"

"It was yoga. You know, the usual—downward dogs and tree poses. It would have been so much better with you there."

"Yeah, I know. I'm sorry about that. It was a crazy week, and I needed this morning just to lounge around with Matt."

"Yeah, sure, whatever. You know, I recall someone who

so desperately wanted me to join yoga she spouted about how it does a body and mind good to de-stress. Now I go more than her."

"You are right, I did say that, but let's just say that Matt does his best to make sure I stay good and de-stressed." I couldn't help but roll my eyes as she giggled.

"How's Matt?" I questioned, doing my best to change the subject.

"He's good." She got quiet for a moment, a soft smile coming to her lips. "I should probably tell you that I think I might be in love." Jenna swooned. "He is just everything I have ever wanted. I seriously have to ask myself what made me wait so long."

I let out a laugh, leaned across the table, and whispered, "You waited because you were convinced that he was a player."

"I did not. That was what you said."

"You are such a liar! I told you to take the chance."

Jenna laughed as she stirred her coffee with her biscotti. "So tell me, how's everything going with Ralph?" Jenna asked, taking a bite of her coffee-soaked treat.

I looked around the cafe and laughed. "Ha, don't ask. The man is all tongue. I can't even fathom what he'd be like in bed because I can barely get past a kiss."

Jenna began laughing uncontrollably. "Oh God, that reminds me of that guy I dated in university. Do you remember? What was his name?"

"Scott. Who wouldn't remember? But now look who you have," I said, raising my eyebrows suggestively. Jenna had started dating Matt, one of our close friends, not too long ago. I'd always thought that they would be perfect for one another and was so glad that they had finally taken the plunge.

"And look how long it took to find him."

"At least you found him. I'm just stuck with tongue," I murmured, crossing my eyes and sticking out my tongue. We both laughed.

Truth was, I had struggled in every relationship I'd had, the longest lasting just over a year and ending just as I had come off the hardest year of my life. I was convinced now more than ever that I was destined to be alone. I had just celebrated my thirtieth birthday and felt that lately my biological clock was ticking, but without a serious relationship, there wasn't much I could do about it.

"What about one of our circle?" Jenna asked, snapping me back to our conversation.

"What about them?" I questioned.

"Well, you say that ultimately you want a baby, right? You don't sound super keen on staying with Roger, or the Tongue as you call him, so, what about one of our circle? It takes all the risk out of it. I mean, you at least know who the guy is, what he looks like, what he is like."

"And we are going to kill that idea right now."

"What? Why?" Jenna asked innocently.

"Because you are being ridiculous." I shook my head. "The whole idea of that is just not going to happen."

"No, I'm not. What about Brent? I think you two would make a lovely couple. Or Shawn. Oooh, or Dave. He has an eight-pack most girls would kill to touch," she said, raising her eyebrows.

"Oh my God, just stop." I laughed, hiding my face in my hands.

The door to the cafe opened, grabbing Jenna's attention, her eyes lighting up at whatever idea she had now.

"What?" I asked, taking a bite of the still-warm blueberry muffin that I'd been craving all week. Jenna's eyes were still trained on whoever had walked through the door and was at the counter. I turned just in time to see the sexy Chase Malone leaning against the counter ordering his morning coffee, and I looked back towards Jenna, seeing a silly grin on her face.

"Why not?" She shrugged, her eyes lighting up like a Christmas tree.

"Why not what?"

"Why not Chase?"

"Why not Chase what?" I could feel my heart start to beat faster at what I hoped she wasn't trying to suggest.

"O.M.G! Pull your head out of the sand. He is as single as they come, and he is not looking to settle down anytime soon. He's hot, sexy, smart... Borrow some of his best swimmers and be done with it."

I almost spit my coffee all over Jenna at her suggestion. "Oh my God, no!" I said, balling my napkin up and throwing it at her.

"What is wrong with that idea?? What girl on the face of this earth wouldn't want a night, or hell better yet, a few nights with Chase Malone. Seriously, out of all the guys, he'd be your best bet. I've heard he is dynamite in the sack."

I looked up towards the counter and saw Chase give us an innocent wave.

"Seriously, Sophie, come on, just do it."

"Seriously, Jenna, just shut up already! He's my best friend," I gritted out in embarrassment just in time for Chase to slide into the booth beside me.

"Good morning, ladies," he greeted, reaching across the table for the sugar. "What are you beauties up to on this beautiful day?"

"Trying to help Sophie solve her relationship crisis."

"Oh my God, shut up!" I said, burying my face in my hands.

Chase looked at me, smiling. "Oh, Soph, you are too cute. You think you have a relationship problem?"

I looked to Jenna for help, since she was the one who'd started this whole conversation. "Go ahead, Sophie, share with Chase." She grinned.

I shrugged and looked at him. "Perhaps."

"Perhaps, Sophie, it's more of an asshole problem," he

said, winking and pinching my outer arm, trying to lighten the mood just as his cell phone went off.

"What's that supposed to mean?" I questioned.

"It means that you need to find a nice boy." He winked, "Well, ladies, I have to run," he announced, "the world of law is awaiting me. See you ladies next week."

"Absolutely, we wouldn't miss it." Jenna grinned.

I glared at Jenna as she watched Chase leave the cafe. When she finally turned her attention back to me, I didn't know whether to laugh or cry. "Seriously? You think this is funny?"

"Oh come on, lighten up. I'm trying to help."

"Okay, okay," I said, laughing and squirming at the same time. "Perhaps you are right. Maybe I just need to find myself a nice man, but not Chase."

"Okay, not Chase. But I'm not going to sleep until we find you someone!" She giggled, shoving the last piece of biscotti in her mouth.

We sat and talked for a good hour after Chase had left, and finally, after parting ways, I decided to take a walk through the park near my house. I loved walking in early spring, listening to the birds chirp and smelling the crisp air. As I walked, I could still hear Jenna's suggestion at the forefront of my mind. As much as I hated to admit it, she did have a point. I was comfortable with my male friends, and I knew them all well, and perhaps Chase wasn't such a bad choice.

I shook the absurd thought from my head, crossed the street, and entered my apartment building. I took the elevator up to the twentieth floor and opened my door. I dropped my purse on the floor just inside the door and slipped my shoes off. I went into the kitchen and poured myself a glass of orange juice and immediately saw the flashing light on my phone. I dialed into my voicemail while taking a drink of the sweet liquid. The first message was from my boss reminding me of a meeting on Monday morning; the second was Ralph.

I drank down the rest of my orange juice and was just about to call Ralph back when my cell phone vibrated in my pocket. Looking down at the screen, I saw Chase had left me a message.

CHASE: WHAT ABOUT RALPH? HE SEEMS LIKE A STANDUP GUY.

I rolled my eyes. Not him now too. I laughed out loud and texted him back.

ME: HE KISSES LIKE A LIZARD!

I smiled, closed the chat window, and dialed Ralph's number. Within twenty minutes, I had gone from being in a lizard kissing relationship to being very single once again. I threw my phone down on the dining room table and rested my head on my arm. I lay there listening to the silence of my apartment, debating on crying or getting up and carrying on with my life. When my phone vibrated against the tabletop, I grabbed it and saw a message from Chase.

CHASE: EWWW THAT IS GROSS. BET THAT SORT OF MAKES YOU WISH YOU COULD GO BACK A FEW YEARS AGO AND PICK ME DOESN'T IT. HAHA JUST KIDDING.

I let out a silent laugh, silently wondering about the exact same thing, and plugged my phone into the charging port, made my way down to my bedroom, and got ready for the rest of my day.

Read Finding Forever with You

A Note from the Author

Dear Readers,

I would like to thank you for taking the time to read *His to Hold*. I hope you enjoyed Mia and Bryce's story. If you did, I would love it if you would drop me a review. Reviews are important to me; I love to hear what my readers think.

About the Author

S.L. Sterling had been an avid reader since she was a child, often found getting lost in books. Today if she isn't writing or plotting, she can be found buried in a romance novel. S.L. Sterling lives with her husband and dog in Northern Ontario.

To keep up to date sign up for my
Newsletter

Visit my
Website

Join my Street Team
Sterlings Silver Sapphires

Other Titles by S.L. Sterling

Standalones

It Was Always You

On A Silent Night

Bad Company

Back to You this Christmas

Fireside Love

Holiday Wishes

All I Want for Christmas

Office Misconduct

The Greatest Gift

Into the Sunset

All American Boys Series

Saviour Boy
The Boy Under the Gazebo

The Malone Brothers

A Kiss Beneath the Stars (The Malone Brothers 1)
In Your Arms (The Malone Brothers 2)
His to Hold
Finding Forever with You

Vegas MMA

Dagger

KB Worlds Everyday Heroes

Constraint